Madcap Mystery

MADCAP MYSTERY

KARIN ANCKARSVÄRD

Translated from the Swedish by
Annabelle MacMillan

Illustrated by Paul Galdone

HARCOURT, BRACE & WORLD, INC., NEW YORK

Originally published in Sweden by Albert Bonniers Förlag under the
title of TAG FAST SNÖGUBBEN!
Library of Congress Catalog Card Number: 62-8343
Printed in the United States of America

F G H I J K L M

CONTENTS

Madcap Mystery

1

WE MEET AGAIN

Ramrod, Knut Seaberg's multicolored boxer—the pet of the entire Coeducational School—was headed for home through the streets of Nordvik. His muscular body moved freely, easily, in utter relaxation. His ears hung down; his skin seemed to lie loosely over his sturdy chest; his paws trod the ground airily, in a free, almost dancing manner. The dry autumn leaves, almost the same color as his coat, whirled around in the air and settled in his path.

Ramrod had followed Knut to school after lunch. Then, down by the bicycle racks, he had remembered an errand of his own and had gone off to the other side of the castle. Knut had whistled and shouted, but to no avail. The last he saw of Ramrod was his small tail—a tail so small that it ended almost before it had begun.

Ramrod spent an hour roaming the town, but now he was on the way home. He made his way across the yard that lay between the two wings of the school building, partly because it was the shortest way home and partly because there was a lovely garden on the other side of the street where he had once come upon a sleeping cat under a gooseberry bush. Ramrod had never forgotten that episode. To be sure, the cat had wakened, but nevertheless . . . !

The fact that Ramrod was crossing the playground did not go unnoticed.

Up on the third floor, Class 4C was studying design in the art room, and Cecilia Acker was sitting by one of the windows. Her legs, crossed under her desk, were long and thin; her head sat atop a thin white neck; her hair was ash-blond. In addition, her hands were long and thin, and with some impatience, she moved her fingertips across her pencils and crayons. She had a high forehead, and her eyes were penetratingly blue. A certain modesty and reserve, a certain quietness and out-of-the-ordinariness, distinguished her.

She did not wear her naturally curly hair in a pony tail, although pony tails had appeared on practically every other girl in the school. Her nails were well manicured, but with colorless polish. Her sweater was a pastel shade, in spite of the fact that peacock blue was *the* color for teen-agers that year.

Now she put two fingers to her chin—there were her dimples!—and her eyes lit up with laughter as she looked down toward the playground.

"Hey, Knut. Ramrod's on the way home now."

A boy with a pug nose and a searching glance turned his

head. Brush haircuts had swept the masculine population of the school by storm. Knut had been the first boy to get such a cut, but it had absolutely nothing to do with his giving in to a fad. He had always been a boy with a scientific bent and he had ascertained that with a brush cut he could shorten the time it took him to get ready for school in the morning by a full forty seconds. He lost no time in going to the barber shop.

Michael had been the very first in the class to get a brush cut *because* it was the latest fashion, but by now he had let it grow out again. At this moment, he got up to sharpen a pencil, a tall boy in a rust-colored jacket and perfectly tailored, well-pressed trousers.

For several minutes the art teacher had been making somewhat bitter statements about the students' work.

"Just what do you think this class period is for anyway? A club where you can indulge in casual recreation? How many really acceptable drawings have any of you managed to get done here in class this semester? Bertil! I haven't seen a single stroke emerge from your hands! Let me see how far you've gotten on the design that was due last Monday!"

As Bertil made his way to the teacher's desk, his seatmate, Ulla, suppressed a giggle. She was a pretty girl, dressed in a black jersey blouse, black slacks, and black flat-heeled slippers.

The few students who were really occupied with the art assignment stopped their work. The others stopped what they were doing at the moment. Cecilia turned away from the window and looked toward the front of the room;

11

Carl Axel and Bengt stopped playing ticktacktoe; and Michael stopped sharpening his pencil. It was evident that the teacher was in no mood for nonsense.

He held Bertil's drawing pad out in front of him. Stifled laughter began to spread like wildfire through the classroom. Everybody knew, of course, what Bertil's "design" looked like!

But the teacher, who at that moment resembled a thundercloud ready to burst, unexpectedly changed his expression. The lines in his forehead smoothed out. Wrinkles of laughter began to appear at the corners of his eyes. And simultaneously the stifled laughter broke out; an explosion of general hilarity shook the room from floor to ceiling.

Bertil, who had been peering out from under an unruly lock of hair, now suddenly lifted his head.

"I guess I may as well hold up the masterwork for general inspection," the teacher said as he lifted the drawing pad above his head. "Did you use your own dog as a model?"

The laughter sank into a sigh of admiration. Bertil had done a charcoal drawing of his poodle, and it had turned out extraordinarily well. This was not just any old poodle that appeared in the drawing; it was Topsy herself, with her head cocked slightly to one side and her coal-black, gleaming eyes focused on some longed-for dog paradise.

"Well, finish the dog portrait," the teacher said curtly. "But then, my boy, listen to what I say. You begin work on your design!"

Bertil returned quietly to his desk. Once again Michael

began to turn the handle of the pencil sharpener. He moved to the rhythm of "The Yellow Rose of Texas," softly singing the words to himself. Cecilia recognized the beat and watched his mouth as he formed the different words. Their eyes met behind the teacher's back.

Carl Axel and Bengt took up their game where they had left off. Ulla made a rough sketch of a new dance skirt that she wanted.

Actually, it was only Bertil who continued to work. His thoughts were with Topsy as he worked cautiously with a piece of charcoal in an attempt to improve a shadow.

Meanwhile, down among the gooseberry bushes in the overgrown garden at the west end of the hill leading up to the school, Ramrod snooped around, his broad black nose

sniffing here and there. He was in the midst of a thicket. He snorted.

There was something strange here in the thicket—something he hadn't expected at all, something metallic. Once again Ramrod snorted. Whatever it was, it certainly wasn't a cat. Furthermore, the bushes seemed unusually full of thorns.

Disappointed, Ramrod backed out. He shook himself so violently that his skin crackled. Then at full speed he took off down the hill.

2

A CHANGED CLASS

Nowadays Class 4C very seldom displayed their feeling of happy comradeship—the rapport that Mrs. Wik, their homeroom teacher, had at one time been so proud of, and rightly so. In the past they had been lively—to excess now and then—but open, easy to reach, and they had possessed a feeling of general camaraderie that communicated itself irresistibly from teacher's desk to students' desks and vice versa.

Now and then Mrs. Wik longed to return to the time when her most pressing problem had been Knut and his passion for animals. She had never dreamed that she would reach the point where she would think back, with anything even remotely approaching affection, to the yellow hamster, the guinea pig, the white rats, and the grass snake that once crawled up onto the map stand. Augustus was the name of the grass snake; he had lived in Knut's pocket much longer than any of his classmates had had any inkling.

But nowadays . . . it was difficult to believe that it was the same class sitting there. Sloppiness, forgetfulness, constant talking—well, these were the things you could expect from boys and girls in their early teens, and you simply had to put up with them and try to keep an even disposition.

But there was something else—something worse. Every teacher knows, naturally, that each class has its own character, its own peculiar countenance, which it turns, at times, on many a long-suffering educator.

Class 4C had become impudent—even more than impudent. There was something uncommunicative and unreliable—something downright nasty—about them these days.

As Mrs. Wik stood in the farthest corner of the room and looked out over her class, she decided that she could pinpoint the exact moment when the change had taken place. Now, in retrospect at least, she knew. It had been the day Mary Beth Evander made her dramatic entrance into the auditorium. At first the other pupils had been suspicious of the new girl, but little by little they were more and more impressed. It was in the middle of the term. She was a transfer student from a girls' boarding school in Switzerland.

The words of wisdom that Mrs. Wik had so often heard —that one newcomer can completely change an entire class—had been proven true.

The girls almost immediately began to sharpen their weapons in the face of Mary Beth's elegant appearance and regal control of every situation. That was to be expected. But you would certainly have supposed that the males in the class would supply a much-needed counterbalance against the tendency of the girls to indulge in unlimited admiration. The boys usually considered it part of their duty to appear superior to and skeptical and suspicious of anything new. A mixed class was always less inclined to exaggerate than was a class composed solely of girls—this Mrs. Wik knew from long experience. She smiled as she thought to herself that a mixed class was quite often a marriage, not as yet very mature, of both benefits and drawbacks. . . .

But the matter of Mary Beth had caused the usually sound judgment of the boys to cease functioning.

Not only was Mary Beth elegant and defiantly sophisticated in a way calculated to bewitch teenagers, but she was also a truly colorful person, bold and nonchalant beyond all belief.

In her most unemotional tone of voice, Mrs. Wik asked Mary Beth Evander to describe the function of the heart ventricles in human beings in regard to the circulation of the blood.

"Go up and get the pointer and show us on the big chart!"

To her own horror, Mrs. Wik felt a terrible dislike for the girl rising within herself. Just the sight of her tailor-made riding habit and her high leather boots—was this

a proper way to dress to come to school?—made the blood
rise to Mrs. Wik's head. She made a desperate effort to
control herself. In this particular class period, Mary Beth
had not yet had the opportunity to display her ignorance.

Mrs. Wik knew, of course, that even a teacher has ob-
scure depths in her own emotions. When she saw Mary
Beth making her way toward the front of the classroom,
more like a fashion model than a pupil in school, she also
knew that every eye in the room was focused upon her
progress, and she saw, moreover, that Mary Beth cast a
glance from under her long eyelashes at Michael—
Michael, of all people!—a glance that had no business in a
schoolroom. Mrs. Wik suddenly exploded. She didn't
bother to ask herself what was the source of this particular
emotion.

"Look here, Mary Beth," she said in a frigid tone of
voice. "Is it absolutely necessary for you to come to school
in a riding habit? It can hardly be healthy for you to sit
through four class periods in those warm leather boots!"

Mary Beth turned her oval face toward the teacher. It
was an almost perfect oval—perhaps a tiny bit broad across
her cheek bones. Her skin was smooth, a trifle dark in
tone, lustrous, and pearl-like—a complexion that had little
to do with winter in the far north.

Her almond-shaped eyes, in keeping with her face,
never changed expression. She answered, "I usually go
around in a riding habit. And I'm going directly to the
riding academy after school. I don't have time to change
clothes in between."

With those words and with her imperturbable calm, which was not put on and which never deserted her, she lifted the pointer from its position. Simultaneously she exchanged another glance—this time with Carl Axel, who was sitting in the second row and who became so confused that he managed to knock his biology book and pencils onto the floor with a clatter and bang.

Mrs. Wik seethed inside. She knew that she had been unwise to have made such a personal observation.

"I think Wicky's completely allergic to Mary Beth," Ulla whispered to Knut.

Knut looked bored to death. He was the only one in the class who hadn't fallen under Mary Beth's spell, and Mrs. Wik had to give him credit for that. It was quite obvious that he felt ill at ease in the face of the changes his classmates had undergone, but he showed his discomfort, unfortunately, by what amounted to his having little or nothing to do with any kind of schoolwork. No longer did he take any part in the daily life of the class. He spent his class periods staring vacantly ahead, no doubt in a world of his own, inhabited by birds of paradise and big game instead of by classmates.

Her face unmoved, Mary Beth studied the diagram of the circulation of the blood, which was fastened to the map rack. After the noise from Carl Axel's desk had subsided, quiet reigned in the room.

Accompanied by a swaying, graceful movement of her whole body, Mary Beth took the pointer and found a speck midway between the heart and the lungs. In a quiet voice she said, "The blood comes from the aorta and passes the ventricles here . . . and here . . ." Once again the swaying motions, this time to a greater degree, whereupon deathly silence ensued.

Mrs. Wik let the quietude settle itself upon her class, long, heavily. Karin Sandberg giggled from pure nervousness. But Mary Beth returned the pointer to its usual place and smiled sweetly at her classmates. Her narrow eyes, showing nothing but the greatest calmness, were focused upon the teacher.

Nervously, Carl Axel shifted from one side of his seat to the other—one . . . two . . . three times before Mrs. Wik broke in.

"Mary Beth, have you even opened the book for today's assignment?" she asked unemotionally.

Promptly and in a clear voice her answer came. It was always that way with her.

"My brother uses the same book, and he forgot to bring it home from school yesterday. My mother thinks it's foolish to buy the same book twice. It's always so expensive with all these new books!"

A wave of half-suppressed laughter swept through the room. The answer was much more insolent than the uninitiated could comprehend. It was downright defiant when you knew that the Evander family lived in one of the largest and most expensive villas in Nordvik, that they had several cars, a number of servants, and several race horses, which were mentioned frequently in the daily papers.

But this time Mrs. Wik managed to stop any observation of a personal nature from escaping from her lips. Instead she went up to her desk, sat down, and took out her grade book.

"That is not a valid excuse and you know it!" she said wearily as she placed her pen on the fullest column in the whole book. "Go sit down! You know, don't you, that you've just gotten your sixth—no, seventh—demerit for this week?"

Mary Beth glided along between the rows of seats. Her well-polished boots glistened. As she passed Michael's desk, she brushed her blue-black hair from her forehead and shrugged her shoulders.

"And furthermore," Mrs. Wik continued as her pen scratched angrily on the paper, "you were supposed to take notes and make your own diagrams of the circulation of the blood in class yesterday. It's dimly possible that you might have learned today's lesson from your own notes. Why didn't you do just that if I may ask?"

With interest, the pupils came to life again. Now how would Mary Beth worm her way out of this?

"Well, Mrs. Wik, a terrible thing happened to my notes. I had forgotten my briefcase yesterday, and I wrote everything on a piece of paper I borrowed. Then I went riding afterwards!"

Mary Beth stood beside her desk. Her words, pronounced indolently and in a drawling, but clear, voice, were swallowed whole by all her classmates. Even Mrs. Wik listened as if hypnotized.

21

"Well, anyway, I was going to buy a new riding ticket —good for ten times, and it costs forty crowns—and I took a fifty-crown note out of my pocket, and of course the piece of paper with the biology notes came out with the money!"

"And you dropped it, naturally!" Mrs. Wik sputtered as she shut her grade book with a bang.

"Oh, no, of course not!" Mary Beth sounded offended. Every face in the room—even Knut's—was turned in her direction. "Just at the moment when I was paying my money with the one hand, I was holding Hell Dog's reins with the other."

Giggles from all directions.

Mrs. Wik opened her mouth but didn't manage to get out a single word before the girl continued.

"I don't see anything so funny about that. His name *is* Hell Dog! Anyway, before I knew what had happened, he had grabbed my biology notes. And he ate them up. Swallowed them whole, for that matter! I was glad that it wasn't the fifty crowns that went down his throat!"

Her last sentence was drowned out by gales of laughter —a merriment that spread through the class with the effectiveness of a hurricane. Hoarse adolescent masculine voices were mixed with the shrill laughter of the girls. Actually, voices as such disappeared; in their place came howling and bellowing.

It was quite a while before Mrs. Wik could make herself heard above the din—and then only by banging the pointer on her desk.

"Mary Beth, what kind of nonsense is that! You should really learn to curb your imagination!"

As though she had been offended at Mrs. Wik's attack on her innocence, she lifted her head and her slim throat with great dignity. But before she had time to say a word, Karin Sandberg unexpectedly stood up at her desk in the first row. She was the president of the class, faithful and ambitious. Herself the daughter of one of the teachers at the school, she usually had an easier time than did the others in understanding the control a teacher must have over her pupils. For this reason it was with both surprise and a feeling of complete helplessness that Mrs. Wik at this moment saw a pair of eyes bright with indignation. The whole of Karin's bearing indicated that she was deeply offended on her classmate's behalf.

"What Mary Beth said is absolutely true! I saw it— everything. I was there! The horse really ate the piece of paper. I think it's . . . it's not very nice to say that Mary Beth is telling a lie without really finding out."

Karin sat down as hastily as she had stood up. She was blushing all the way up to the roots of her hair, and she probably felt that she had said too much. But a collective murmur of approval showed that the class was behind her 100 per cent.

For a couple of seconds Mrs. Wik sat in silence.

Just how far could this go? Animosity and contempt had replaced the usual friendliness and feeling of comradeship. She was aware that she could give them another lecture, begging them to keep in mind that they were now in the fourth class, that their grades in the spring would be decisive in the question of their admission to advanced schooling, and that the achievements of the class were sinking to a lower and lower level with each passing month. She could have spoken of all the precious time they were wasting in class periods by endless discussions and interruptions of this sort.

But she also knew that her words would fall on deaf ears. No one would pay the slightest attention to her.

"Sit down, Mary Beth," she said sharply. "We don't have time to discuss your adventures in class. You have obviously not managed to do your assignments—as usual. . . . Knut, quickly. Circulation of the blood!"

When Mrs. Wik returned to her favorite place—the corner of the room—she noticed Karin whispering eagerly, anxiously, to her seatmate, Hans Karlberg, and she observed the smile of triumph on Mary Beth's face—true to form.

But she also noticed something else.

Back there in her seat by the window, Cecilia Acker was leaning her head on her hands. She kept her face toward the blackboard, but her clear blue eyes were somewhere else. They looked beyond Mary Beth with a curious expression—simultaneously watchful, searching, contemplative.

In her expression was neither joy nor compassion, neither enthusiasm nor admiration. Her glance was so sober, so skeptical, so mature that in its solitude it cut like a sword through the confusion in the room.

25

Cecilia, fragile and modest, didn't really belong among those pupils Mrs. Wik usually paid attention to, but now it suddenly occurred to her that here, in the midst of all the fuss over Mary Beth, sat a young lady who took no part in the proceedings but who didn't miss a trick.

3

MICHAEL AND HIS REPUTATION

At the end of the school day, the narrow roads leading down from the school hill were completely congested with traffic. At one time long ago, they had seemed wide to the previous generations who wore black school caps and who had never known the lure of speed, but now, with more and more cars each year, each month, each day, the narrow streets became traffic bottlenecks. In the rows of bicycles and motor scooters, there was something wild and elemental as they hurried from the schoolyard, every mind beset with the same idea—to get out and away as swiftly as possible. On these occasions, even the most hardened truck drivers were content to stop at the foot of the hill and wait for the flood of traffic to subside.

Quickest among the quick and boldest among the bold was Michael—and not without reason, at least three days a week. His classes finished at twenty minutes to three,

and as early as three o'clock he had to be at what he
proudly called his "place of employment"—Nordvik's
lumberyard, on the other side of the overgrown garden
below the school. There he spent two hours sorting pieces
of lumber, and every cent he earned went into his piggy
bank, an old cracker box that he kept hidden in the inner
recesses of his closet. With the addition of some money
he had gotten for Christmas and for his birthday, the sum
in the cracker box was close to three hundred crowns.

He would soon have reached the halfway point in his
goal—the magic sum of eight hundred crowns, the price
of the shining, glistening article in the window of the
Nordvik Hardware and Sport Company, the thought of
which occupied him every waking hour. A motor scooter.

Michael calculated that with perseverance and thrifti-
ness—Cecilia called it outright, unmitigated stinginess—
the sum would reach eight hundred crowns at precisely
the right moment psychologically—that is to say, just
about the time he would have his fifteenth birthday.

There were days, of course, when he sensed a certain
emptiness in not having a minute to exchange words with
his friends after school, and at times it was actually irritating to see Knut and Carl Axel and the others disappear
down in the direction of the football field. But he needed
only to let his thoughts drift to the light blue motor
scooter in all its beauty, to hear, with his inner ear, the
motor sputter once . . . twice . . . catch hold, whir,
accelerate.

And on this particular day he was more lost than usual,

deep in his dream of the motor scooter. He stood outside the Dairy Store and gulped down, ravenously, methodically, four sweet rolls. This took him exactly five minutes and was a part of his promise to his worried mother, who, as mothers usually do, concerned herself about his possible bad grades, overexertion, sickness, and other miscellaneous ailments that could result from extra work. Michael actually credited his mother with good sense and excellent judgment—in anything that had nothing to do with him.

Without protest he conscientiously ate the rolls every day, partly because he was truly hungry and partly because, by buying rolls instead of other popular snacks, he was able to save eight cents—which, of course, went straight into the cracker box.

As he stood there, Cecilia passed by. She waved at him with one of those hasty, almost childish motions that seemed so natural for her.

Michael mused that she really looked very sweet. The sky-blue color of the scarf on her head reminded him of the motor scooter.

Not far behind Cecilia came Mary Beth, bicycling along with Carl Axel and Hans, one on each side. Her scarf, the color of the autumn leaves, highlighted the blue tones in her shiny jet-black hair.

She didn't bother to wave; she stopped.

"Oh, Michael! You aren't going down to that stupid, idiotic old lumberyard again, are you? Why don't you come along to the stables with me!"

29

Mary Beth pursed her lower lip and dragged down the corners of her mouth.

Carl Axel and Hans both looked embarrassed.

Mary Beth could pout in such a way as to guarantee discomfort to anyone in the immediate vicinity.

"That's a hot one!" Michael said curtly.

Then he looked at Mary Beth's hair, which flew in the wind, at her pouting mouth. He noticed that she looked disappointed, and he thought that was very nice of her.

"I can come with you some other time!" he said by way of consolation. "Maybe some Saturday."

Mary Beth nodded and glanced at him with great understanding—something that Michael didn't notice but that, to a large degree, provoked both Carl Axel and Hans.

And on the other side of the street was Ann, Cecilia's eleven-year-old sister. She snorted contemptuously.

"Look. Isn't it nauseating?" she whispered to her best friend Eva. "They can't even see through what she's trying to do!"

Deep in thought, Eva chewed her gum wildly for a few seconds before she answered.

"I just don't understand what they see in her," she said as she glanced disapprovingly at Mary Beth and her two escorts, who disappeared around a bend in the street. "She looks so dopey, too. And have you seen that brother of hers—a tall, repellent character in the fifth class?"

"Is he just in the fifth class?"

"Yes. Peter is his name. I saw him yesterday in their big car. He was driving, but I'll bet you anything he isn't anywhere near eighteen years old, and there was a woman beside him. A platinum-blond number, can you imagine! And old. Wouldn't surprise me if she were *twenty!*"

The two small schoolgirls, in their duffel coats, shook their heads so wildly that their pony tails waved in the breeze.

Michael gulped down the last bite of the fourth roll and took his bicycle out of the rack. Just as he was about to put one foot on the pedal, he halted as someone called out his name.

In surprise, he turned around, because the voice that had called his name was the heavy voice of a man, and, strangely enough, something inside him jumped when he heard it. A dim memory stirred in his subconscious.

Striding briskly across the street was Inspector Nilsson of Nordvik's police.

"Michael Olmstedt! The very person I've been thinking about. Hi, there, Michael. What are you up to these days?"

Somewhat embarrassed, Michael bowed slightly. His hand, although long and narrow, disappeared completely in the mighty grip of the inspector. Michael blushed clear up to the edge of his cap, and suddenly he didn't look a day over fourteen years of age.

"Oh, I go to school—and I'm also working at the lumberyard now and then in the afternoons. To earn a little pin money!"

"Well, what do you know about that? I thought you were relatively wealthy with all the reward money you got when you were helping me!" said the inspector with a grin.

Michael smiled, but not without some embarrassment.

However, he managed to bring the situation under control.

"Oh, I still have that money," he explained. "But I'm not allowed to use it for just any old thing. Right now I'm saving money to buy a motor scooter. I have to be at the lumberyard at three o'clock," he added after sneaking a quick look at his wrist watch.

"Oh, well, then you've got to hurry," said Inspector Nilsson. "But there's something I'd very much like to discuss with you. I can walk with you part of the way."

"Get a load of that!" whispered Ann to Eva, and her pony tail almost stood straight up in the air. "The inspector and Michael. Take my word for it—there's something funny going on again. That guy Michael has a fantastic talent for getting himself involved with all sorts of things."

Eva nodded.

"I wonder what's up now? But maybe they're only reminiscing over old memories."

They both giggled, and the more they giggled, the funnier they thought the whole business of Michael and the inspector.

At length they were completely helpless with laughter, to the point where they couldn't stand up, and they clung, instead, either to each other or to each other's bicycle.

Michael and his companion ambled slowly along the road where the October daylight, waning, uncertain, filtered down between the tops of the maple trees and made the gravel on the path seem golden and almost waxy.

"It's been a long time since we had much to do with each other!" the inspector remarked as he looked down at Michael.

The inspector was an enormously tall, strong blond man with small, narrow eyes. His expression had a curious blankness—almost reminiscent of absent-mindedness—about it. Michael remembered this not without a shiver of excitement. He knew that few people in this world were equipped with such keen powers of observation as was Inspector Nilsson.

"So, you're working at the lumberyard. I knew that, of course, and it's just because of that fact that I wanted to get in touch with you," he said unexpectedly. "How do you like it?"

"Oh, it's fine!" Once again Michael felt a bit confused and fingered his bicycle bell nervously. He realized that the policeman had noticed his nervousness, and he stopped playing with the bell. "By that I mean that it's O.K. I can't say that it's an *intriguing* job in any way. Usually I sort lumber, and now and then I get sent on errands. Actually, it's kind of monotonous, of course, but most everything—at least, jobs that are open to students—is nowadays!"

The inspector smiled.

"Oh, I wouldn't say that. There's a whole lot going on nowadays!" he said. "And it's for this reason that I thought of you just recently. You can't have escaped hearing a lot of talk about all the robberies that have been committed in the last few weeks!"

"Robberies?"

"Don't you read *The Nordvik Herald?* For that matter, there's been something about them almost every day in the city newspapers, too. Where have you been keeping yourself?"

"In school and at the lumberyard!" Michael's adolescent voice cracked just at that moment, and the statement came out with such force that a squirrel, frightened to the point of panic, shot up the nearest tree and immediately offered up a prayer of thanks that he had escaped with his life.

"Tell me about it, Inspector. Please do."

"Most of the robberies have taken place in newsstands. But a couple of them have been in private houses, and in these cases the thieves have wantonly destroyed a lot of property and messed things up in general. Actually, the only thing they seem to have been after was liquor, and in both cases the value was considerable. From the newsstands they have usually taken mostly cigarettes. The total value of what they have stolen is no trifling sum, I can tell you. At least six of the newsstand robberies have been the work of the same person—or persons."

"But all of the newsstand robberies can't have taken place in Nordvik! There aren't that many stands in the whole town, are there?" Michael asked in a tone so professional that it would have amused Cecilia highly had she been there to hear him.

"Two of them have been here in Nordvik," the inspector continued. "The others have taken place in the surrounding towns. One evening we got reports on two robberies less than two miles from each other."

"In that case, they must have had a car."

"A car or some other fast means of transportation. But there's something extraordinary about the whole business. In most cases where robbery is concerned, we almost always get a report on an auto theft in the neighborhood, and in that way we can usually track down the thieves. Fairly often we find the car smashed up somewhere a few miles from the scene of the robbery. But with these recent robberies, we haven't had any such clues to help us. The thefts don't seem to be very well planned. In fact, they seem to be on the spur of the moment. In the private houses, the thieves have ignored expensive jewelry and silverware and have concentrated on liquor. They've taken every bottle in sight. Strangely enough, they've also taken all the bottles of soft drinks—Coca-Cola, for example— that were around. This is why we're convinced that these robberies are the work of some gang of boys who live around here."

Michael began to walk a little faster; time was slipping away. They had reached the old overgrown vacant lot. Behind the old apple trees, where bees and hornets swarmed around half-rotten frostbitten apples, they could see the well-kept buildings and long, narrow sheds belonging to the lumberyard.

"Why do you say from around here?"

"Otherwise, I don't think they would have bothered with so many petty crimes in such a small district. Rather,

I think they would have gone some place new every time. Here in this area, everyone is on guard constantly. We suspect, you see, that the thieves haven't anything but bicycles—or, perhaps, motor scooters—at their disposal and that, for this reason, they can't operate in a wider area."

"Isn't it possible that they have the use of a car once in a while? Maybe they simply appropriate someone's car and get it back before anyone has noticed."

"No, that isn't impossible at all," Inspector Nilsson said. "In any case, we're pretty sure we aren't dealing with professional criminals. We can usually trace them through the various receivers of stolen goods whose names are in our files. But in these cases that we're dealing with now, we can be helped immeasurably by the general public if they only keep their eyes open. That's why I thought of you, Michael. You know most of the young fellows here in Nordvik. And you don't usually go through life half asleep! If I remember correctly, you don't even sleep much at night."

Both of them laughed. Again Michael blushed in embarrassment. He realized that he was blushing, and in order to make his awkwardness a little less conspicuous, he gave one of the rotten apples a mighty kick. It flew in an arch over what remained of the barbed wire fence that had once encircled the vacant lot.

Two seconds later, both Michael and Inspector Nilsson were out in the middle of the road. A monstrous animal, about the size of a calf, shot out from the bushes.

The only noise up to this moment had been the buzzing

36

of the bees and hornets. This sudden disturbance seemed to make the heavens ring.

"Bo-o-o-ow, wowowowowowowowow!"

"What in heaven's name . . . ?" cried the inspector. He wasn't prepared for an attempt at assassination on the streets of Nordvik.

Suddenly two heavy gray paws came flying at Michael's chest, and a soft, rosy pink tongue began to lick his face. He staggered but managed to regain his balance.

"Hey, Ramrod! Look, take it easy, will you? It's only the Seaberg's dog, Inspector. He's always down here snooping around among the bushes. Down, Ramrod. Down!"

Ramrod, who by now felt that he had gotten his sweet revenge for the rotten apple that had hit him right on the forehead, began to sniff at Inspector Nilsson's trouser leg. He wagged his tail furiously.

Michael, of course, was an old friend.

As far as the policeman was concerned, it looked as if the dog were thinking, "I don't recognize you, but I guess you're all right."

"I have to run," Michael announced. "But I promise that I'll keep my eyes and ears open."

The inspector gave him a quick glance.

"There are quite a few of you fellows working at the lumberyard, aren't there? Weren't there a couple of new employees just this fall?"

Michael, who had removed his cap, remained standing there, cap in hand.

"Up there in the lumberyard?" he said. "Yes, there are a few new guys. But they're nice fellows, all of them. Well, good-by now, Inspector."

38

Michael bowed somewhat hesitantly, far from sure as to how he could end the conversation.

"I'll see you around, Michael." Jokingly the inspector gave Michael a salute and went on his way with brisk, assured steps.

In contrast, Michael's steps, as he walked his bicycle along, were slow and hesitant. The policeman's last words had left a somewhat bitter taste in his mouth.

4

OUT UNDER THE STARS

When the bold, merciless winter puts down its first blanket of frost over the meadows and gardens, when the half-light of day becomes a dark blue curtain as early as four o'clock in the afternoon, the wondrous feeling of having a home is better than at almost any other time of year. It's good to shut the gate down by the road, to shut the front door against the chilly weather, to shut your own door against a dark corridor.

And you can't get away from the fact, either, that the feeling of well-being is heightened if you aren't alone—if you have a four-footed pal for company.

Ramrod had caught up with Knut right outside the Seaberg's house, and for a good while both of them indulged in long, involved ceremonies of greeting. At least a dozen times Ramrod tried to run between Knut's legs. They even attempted to dance a tango right in the middle of the street. Knut's long, intimate acquaintance with animals had made him completely insensitive to all critical comments from the human race.

At this point he was sitting in his room reading a fascinating book about the animal life in French Equatorial Africa; two liverwurst sandwiches and a Coca-Cola were within easy reach.

And there, in an ancient, worn-out armchair, which Knut himself had bought at an auction, lay Ramrod, luxuriously stretched out. Both his paws and his head hung down from the edge of the chair, but his back was well supported, and it was obvious that Ramrod was just as pleased with his chair as Knut was with French Equatorial Africa.

Outside the darkness was coming thick and fast. It was warm and cozy in the room. Knut, the dog, the book, and, in addition, a bluish-green aquarium were all together in the circle of light from the lamp. From the aquarium flashed bits of gold and red among the bubbles.

What was it that caused everything to change? What kind of summons was this, not sent by means of sound, that reached the inner core of the dog, even in his deepest sleep?

It all began when Ramrod began to stiffen his paws and his legs. No longer were they dangling carelessly from the chair. His nose began to quiver; his pink tongue appeared at one corner of his black mouth. He didn't change position, but both of his huge, shiny brown eyes were wide open. They seemed to look into the distance—far, far away —where no human eye could focus. He needed no book to

41

recognize the summons to the unknown, the tempting, fraught with danger.

Suddenly he jumped to the floor. He shook himself; he stretched himself premeditatedly and ceremoniously. Not for a second did he take his eyes off Knut, who was undoubtedly aware of the symptoms but who didn't really want to be disturbed.

More stretching. A deep yawn.

"Go lie down, Ram! Down!"

Ramrod sat down. For about five seconds he remained seated. Then he rushed to the door. He snorted and pawed at the door. Knut gave him an angry look.

"Look, you've been out almost the whole day! It's pitch dark and cold as the dickens out there!"

Ramrod whined softly. His whole body, so relaxed just a few moments previously, was as tense as a spring.

Knut put down his book and glanced at the clock. Almost five o'clock.

Of course there was always the possibility that the dog really *did* need to go out. Knut looked at him suspiciously. He had seen him this way before.

Ramrod had a good home with Knut. He was the proud possessor of a fine leather neckband on which was his tax tag and Knut's telephone number. He had his own chair and, in addition, a big basket with a cushion and a blanket. Without a moment's loss of dignity, he had allowed himself to be displayed at dog shows, where his behavior could only be described as pompous.

But there were occasions in his life when the world of

human beings simply didn't interest him.

Knut caught sight of the sad, dejected look in Ramrod's eyes.

Just a few minutes ago it had all been so nice, so comfortable.

Knut closed the book and opened the door.

Ramrod tore down the steps like a wild animal who has just been let out of chains. His feet were heavy as they hit the stone floor of the vestibule.

"Stay here in the neighborhood, do you hear?" Knut said seriously. But, in any case, he opened the door.

Twilight was a thing of the past. Darkness was so thick that it seemed to hit one in the face as it swept across Nordvik.

Knut whistled admonishingly. He hoped that Ramrod would just take his usual swing down by the fence and around the lilac bushes and would then come bounding back into the half-open door.

But he miscalculated. The dog barked wildly a couple of times—overjoyed to be free. Then the darkness swallowed him up.

Knut listened. Knut whistled. He listened some more. But the dog had disappeared just like a phantom. In the solitary darkness, there wasn't a sound to be heard—not even the crackling of dry branches. Far, far away you could hear the whistle on the Nordvik train.

The cold weather, earlier than usual and quite unexpected, was as heavy as a suit of armor encompassing the whole of nature's realm. On evenings like this, the waves in the bay tumbled roughly as if they were terrified of becoming frozen over.

In his shirt sleeves, Knut began to shiver from the cold. Angrily he shut the door. He was disturbed over having let himself be tricked again!

By this time Ramrod was far away. Silently but swiftly he ran down a path—a path known only to him. It was dark, but, after all, there were the stars.

This was no path that followed along one of Nordvik's streets or roads; it led through the bushes where the blackbirds spent their lazy hours, past the place where the porcupine hid under an old heap of stones, over a rocky ledge where the fox had his den.

There were many things in this world of which Knut had no knowledge.

Ramrod hurried across the fields at Ekenase and ran through the reeds along the shore. The moon was coming up, round and smooth, over the bay, and the sheer joy of being alive pulsed wildly in the dog's flexible body.

It would have been impossible to follow him on his happy journey under the stars. Equally impossible would it have been to count up the seconds, the minutes, the hours . . .

About the time everyone in Nordvik was ready to go to bed, after glancing unhappily at the mercury, which, with every passing moment, seemed to be going lower and lower, Ramrod found himself in the overgrown vacant lot down below the school. It was usually fun to play here. Was the cat perhaps sleeping under her favorite bush? The frisky squirrels, the fleet-footed weasel, or the huge, fat rabbit who just couldn't say no to a delicious apple?

Ramrod rummaged around in the thicket.

No cat. No rabbit.

But quiet! What was that?

Ramrod's whole body stiffened. In his delight and antic-ipation, one forepaw remained suspended in mid-air.

It was the sound of automobile wheels in the gravel. Someone turned on a flashlight.

Ramrod's sensitive nose began to quiver. Suddenly he had the scent. People! Terribly quiet people, though. The sounds didn't tell him much, even though his ears were standing straight up.

Oh, but there was something! Rattling. Jingling. A door. The squeak of a rusty lock.

Overcome by curiosity, Ramrod took two or three hesi-tant steps out of the thicket.

Starlight was such a friendly thing! The moon was so delightfully round! And there, somewhere nearby, lived the rabbit, the blackbirds, and the squirrels. But they weren't at home, or, if they were, they weren't in the mood to play. But maybe these people would do.

Soft whispers were heard. A girl giggled. There were various hushed voices—the creaking voices of adolescent boys.

Ramrod *loved* the creaky voices. They were just like Knut's, and Knut was the greatest guy in the world!

Excitedly he jumped out from the bushes—just at that point where he had bumped his nose on something hard a few days before. He barked—the happy sort of bark that means, "Hey, don't you want to play?"

45

However, the only answer was a scream.

The voices grew excited.

"What the Sam Hill?"

"Darned old dog!"

Ramrod howled piercingly. Something terribly hard had hit his soft, sensitive nose.

"Just a friendly dog. But, for heaven's sake, shut him up. He'll wake up . . . !"

Something sharp, thrown with enormous force, hit Ramrod's head. He howled wildly again. He saw red; he saw black; and thick clouds fell before his eyes.

He tottered. Then he fell, rolling over on one side. The dry, dead branches crackled.

But all the while the stars glittered, brittle and sharp as diamonds, and shone down on the Nordvik houses and grounds. The moon continued to shine through the tree-tops.

5

NOCTURNAL DRAMA AT THE ACKER HOUSE

Cecilia stretched out in bed. The sheets felt fresh and clean. She read a few more pages in her magazine. Mechanically her eyes went back and forth over the lines of print, but she was barely conscious of what the words said.

" 'Desperate Tina' is five feet three inches tall and weighs one hundred and forty-nine pounds. Well, my dear, you really ought to try to lose a number of pounds. But don't try to do it too quickly. Avoid . . .' "

Cecilia went back a few lines. Five feet three inches and one hundred and forty-nine pounds! Heavenly days! What a butterball!

She smiled to herself, but the smile was soon drowned in the wave of an enormous yawn. Slowly she let the magazine slide to the floor. For a couple of minutes she lay there, her eyelids heavy, looking at the little pleated shade on the wall lamp. She loved the small rosebuds painted on the shade. Then she reached out and turned off the lamp.

She curled up like a cat.

Five feet three inches! Why, she was a full four inches taller and didn't weigh more than one hundred and twenty-three pounds. Her thoughts, already disjointed like the individual pieces of a jigsaw puzzle, faint and rosy-colored, drifted to measurements once again. She was perfectly contented. Mary Beth weighed one hundred and thirty-one.

With one final endeavor to keep awake, Cecilia opened her eyes. Yes, just as she had thought! There was a full moon. Through the small panes of her window, the moon-light filtered into the room, grazing the filmy curtains, creating a ribbon-wide strip of light on her green-and-white-striped bedspread.

Math . . . in the . . . morning . . . that last number . . . was it one hundred and forty-nine pounds? . . . no . . . it was teaspoons . . . pennies . . .

It all began with a small rustling sound from the window. Cecilia, accustomed to the utter silence of the Nordvik night, turned her head in her sleep. Her light hair spread out over the pillow like a gigantic fan.

There were the rustling sounds again—and another sort of weak sound. Deep in sleep, Cecilia sighed.

Rustle, rustle. Then a reverberating plop against the window sill. At this point Cecilia opened her eyes. Not yet quite conscious, she stared at the stream of moonlight, which had moved all the way to the top of the sheet.

More rustlings—the unmistakable sound of a piece of gravel thrown at the pane. Cecilia's heart began to pound. She sat straight up in bed.

Someone was throwing sand or gravel at her window! Was it possible that some member of her family had gotten locked out?

Before Cecilia had gotten halfway across the floor, she remembered that Ann had come home from the library at eight o'clock and had put the chain on the door.

Who could it be at this time of night?

Cecilia threw the window open. The whole side of the house was bathed in moonlight, but the gravel path below was just a dark patch of nothing. It was frosty and cold. In no time she was shivering.

"What is it? Is someone down there?"

After a moment she could see a couple of figures in the darkness. One of them moved. It even talked.

"Hey, Cecie! Are you awake?"

She had been roused out of a deep sleep. She snorted.

"Awake? Of course, I'm awake. Do you think I'd be standing here otherwise?"

"It's me. Knut. Let me in, please. Ramrod has been hurt. Do you have any bandages in your house?"

Cecilia opened her mouth. She was so cold that her teeth chattered. She was on the verge of making a few sarcastic comments, but she stopped herself. She also had the feeling that one of the dark shadows down there —probably Ramrod—was unusually, terribly still.

49

"Wait," was all she said. "I'll come down and unlock the door."

In her long red bathrobe and her slippers, she hurried down the stairs. Not until she was in the downstairs hall did she put on any lights, because she decided that she had better hear Knut's story first. If, in addition to herself, her curious, snoopy little brothers, to say nothing of her astonished mother and father, woke up and decided to come down and investigate, the whole situation would be completely unbearable.

Her fingers quaking, Cecilia took off the chain, turned the key in the lock, and opened the door.

A strange, sad creature staggered into the hall, followed by Knut.

It was Ramrod. He seemed to be bleeding profusely near one of his eyes; his whole body shook, either because of the cold or the fright or both. Wound around his neck was Knut's striped scarf, an English import, famous throughout the class for its great length. In spite of the fact that the scarf was wound around his neck several times, it dragged on the floor, and the dog stumbled over it with each step he took. With his good eye, which was just as shiny and brown and friendly as always, he looked trustingly, first at Cecilia, then at Knut.

Cecilia put two fingers to her chin. "Oh, Knut!" she said.

Immediately she knelt down beside Ramrod and put both her arms around his neck.

Knut viewed the scene with approval. Ramrod sat down and gave Cecilia a wet but faint lick on her ear.

Slowly the blood continued to drop from his forehead, down onto the polished parquet floor.

"It was like this, you see," Knut began. He put his cap under his arm and squatted down beside Cecilia. "Ramrod has gone absolutely crazy over a lady boxer on the other side of the castle. It's that dog named Cleo—you know, the Ekholms' dog. He might as well move over there. Every single night I have to chase down there and get him. Well, I went down there tonight—or, in reality, last night—the same as usual. But he wasn't there. I thought he'd come eventually, so I went home. When I had gotten about halfway home—right there by that overgrown vacant lot down below the school, you know—I heard some strange sounds. Small whines. I went into the bushes, and there I found Ram. He was lying under the bushes. At first I thought he was dead.

"But then I could see that he was breathing. I guess he recognized the smell of me, because his nose began to quiver. In a little while he got up—onto his hind legs first, and then onto his front legs. But he was absolutely groggy. I could see that he was bleeding—although his eye isn't as bad as it looks—and then I remembered that you lived close by. It's a long way from here to my house, as you know."

"Poor, poor Ramrod!" Cecilia whispered as she let her light hair fall across the dog's wrinkled forehead. "Poor, poor dog!"

At that moment she stiffened. Lights were turned on upstairs. Above the banister could be seen unruly light hair and a wide-open mouth.

"Oh, dear," Cecilia said in a hushed voice. "They've all waked up."

Further proof of her words came when a door opened on the other side of the hall. There on the threshold stood Ann in her striped pajamas; her hair was up in curlers. She looked utterly confused.

"What in the world are you doing out here in the middle of the night? What have you done to the dog? What's going on?" The latter question in a loud, agitated tone of voice.

Knut brushed the hair out of his eyes. Cecilia opened her mouth but realized that there simply was nothing she could say.

Two white-blond heads could be seen from the top of the stairs. From the middle of the house came Mrs. Acker's voice.

"Why are Erik and Henrik running around? Hasn't Cecilia gone to bed yet? It's after midnight. Is that girl completely crazy?"

"Uh huh!" Cecilia said drily. "Now you can see for yourself that we have a big family!"

"But, Cecilia, honey!" At last Mrs. Acker had appeared and had surveyed the situation in the hall. "Henrik! Erik! *Don't go down there with your cats!*"

Upon hearing these words, Knut got a good grip on Ramrod's collar. In utter fascination he observed Cecilia's two little brothers, four and six years old respectively, solemnly coming down the stairs, each with a cat tucked tenderly under his arm.

"They ought to be shot. The boys, I mean. Not the cats,"

Cecilia mumbled half aloud. She continued a bit louder, "Get out of here, you kids, and go on to bed!"

"What are their names?" Knut asked. He was an only child, and this lively, noisy household fascinated him because it was such a contrast to his own home.

"His name is Alley!" Erik said, flattered by Knut's attention.

"And his name is Kat!" Henrik said.

And in chorus, they said, "Put them together and they are called Alleykat."

"Why are you standing around here in the middle of the night?" Ann continued obstinately. "What is it?"

"Thursday!" Cecilia sputtered in exasperation.

"The dog's bleeding!" Erik blurted out, and from pure fright dropped Kat who, after a quick, concentrated look at Ramrod's enormous frame, ran right into the fireplace and disappeared up the chimney.

Alley still in his arms, Erik remained extraordinarily unconcerned. He looked Knut up and down from top to toe. Then he lifted his clear, childish voice and, lisping badly, gave his comments on the events of the evening.

"You're Knut, aren't you? You're the guy Cecilia likes nextest bestest after Michael."

The lost cat was immediately forgotten.

Ann snorted loudly.

Cecilia's cheeks became beet-red, and Mrs. Acker felt compelled to break in quickly, though she was conscious that what she was going to say constituted a complete *non sequitur*.

"Your dog must have gotten hurt somewhere. . . .

What time is it anyway? Erik! Henrik! Into bed. Right this very minute!"

In all the confusion she had failed to notice that the youngest Acker, a gentleman with a mind of his own, although he was not much over a year old, had, true to form, felt compelled to appear on the scene. He had heard voices. Before they knew what was happening, he began to come down the stairs backwards. There was no stopping him. He progressed by using one leg to propel himself; he held the other leg curved under himself, more or less as a shock absorber and for protection. He had gotten all the way down to where Knut and Ramrod were before anyone noticed him.

Finally even Cecilia's father appeared in his bathrobe and pajamas at the top of the stairs. In a hushed voice he asked what had happened, but his words were drowned out by Erik, who had, in the meantime, crept over to the fireplace and was trying to climb up after the cat. He shouted ceaselessly.

Henrik, a practical soul who never let a situation get out of control if he could help it, decided that it was the perfect time to inform his mother that his shoelace had broken in three pieces and that he couldn't use it one minute longer.

"You can tie knots in it, of course," he said in a voice that betrayed his many years of practice at drowning out everybody else in the family. "Tie knots in it, sure, but then the knots come between the holes, and you can't get them through the holes, and so the shoestring doesn't really do much good."

"Now, listen. All of you," Cecilia broke in. "Even the Primeval Brat has had to come down and get his two cents' worth in. Get out of here—every last one of you. Get out of here. Can't you hear what I said?"

This was the big sister speaking. And the sparks in her eyes were flying so wildly that the impossible happened. The members of the family began to withdraw from the scene. Henrik slowly went up the stairs sideways, with the half-smothered Alley under one arm, all the while muttering that he *never* got any new shoes, let alone a new *shoelace!*

Humming softly at first and finally singing to herself, Ann lifted the baby into her arms and disappeared with him. What she was singing was, of course:

"If it's like this to be in love when you are little,
Then what's it like in love when you are grown?"

Cecilia was convinced, however, that the tune wasn't quite correct enough for Knut to recognize it.

"There's no doubt that Cecilia will take care of Ramrod," said Mrs. Acker. "Try to wash the dirt out of the sore. You know where all the stuff you'll need is. And then give the poor thing a little water, won't you? Oh, I almost forgot. What a good thing! The bone from last Sunday's roast is still in the refrigerator. Give that to the poor dog, too!"

She disappeared in order to put an end to the confusion in the direction of the nursery.

Cecilia's father, who in imperturbable quietness weathered the storms of daily life in the Acker household, let his fingers move gently around the wound on Ramrod's head.

"This is a deep wound," he declared. "I think you ought to take him to the veterinarian tomorrow and find out if he doesn't need some stitches. This isn't any dog bite. It looks to me as if someone threw a sharp stone at him. But fortunately, the eye isn't hurt. It's just a patch of skin that is swollen over his eye, and that's what makes it look so terrible. I can tell you, Knut, he's a fine dog with a good disposition."

There were several occasions that night when Ramrod proved that he was, indeed, a fine dog with a good disposition. Knut and Cecilia took him up to the bathroom and, with great care, washed the wound with a disinfectant. This was painful, and Ramrod whined softly, but he sat as still as a statue, strangely enough.

"He knows that we're only taking care of him," Knut said as he watched Cecilia's long fingers moving quickly and purposefully.

Their mutual efforts in putting a bandage on the dog were not in the least successful. The patient protested so violently that they had to give up. Knut's striped scarf had to serve once again as it had before.

After they had cared for his wound, they treated Ramrod royally in the Acker kitchen. Knut and Cecilia ate some hard bread and cheese and shared a Coca-Cola as they sat at the kitchen table.

"Then you don't think that he got in a dog fight?" Cecilia asked. She noticed that the object responsible for all the confusion of the evening had, under the magic influence of the bone from the roast, managed to regain his equilibrium.

Knut shook his head as he chewed and swallowed.

"No, I felt just the same as your father did when I found the dog there. He isn't exactly a dwarf, so he must have gotten a terrific blow on the head to have conked out that way there in the bushes. Naturally, he has rivals over Cleo—that's obvious—and I have to admit that he has been in various squabbles with a dog whose name is Dandy and with others. They sit around growling at each other under the hedge over there by Ekholms' house, and now and then they chase each other around. But all the dogs know each other, and they know that Ramrod is by far the strongest, so the squabbles are never very serious. No, this is something else entirely. In the morning I'll go back down there and see if I can find any clues—the stone that hit him in the head, maybe."

"Talk to Michael," Cecilia advised. "He's very good at tracking down all sorts of things, I can tell you!"

It was after one o'clock when she followed her nocturnal visitors out to the hall. From the living room came some sort of rhythmic bumping, which made Ramrod stiffen every muscle in his body. Knut held the leash firmly as he listened.

"What's that? Is someone in there?"

"Hah," Cecilia said with a giggle. "You know perfectly well what that is. It's Kat. He's come down out of the chimney and now he's washing himself."

Knut, who was not usually one to show his feelings to

58

any extent, suddenly gave a loud guffaw as he thought about the events of the evening.

"Your little brothers are really something!" he said with a hint of envy in his voice. "What was it you called the smallest one? Primeval Brat, or something like that? Why did you call him that?"

"Because he's the prototype of all the impossible little babies in the world. He's all of them rolled into one," Cecilia answered as she opened the door. "Well, so long. See you in the morning. And, Ramrod! You get well, do you hear?"

Through the small latticed window in the door she saw the boy and the dog disappear. The dog's head, bandaged with the long scarf, seemed grotesque and huge in the moonlight, which was still bathing the whole of Nordvik in its white light. The boy and the dog were walking so close together that they bumped into each other with every step they took. This looked very peculiar, but Cecilia understood they wanted it that way. It gave them both the security they needed.

6

MID-TERM EXAMINATIONS

During morning recess Knut told Michael all about Ramrod's adventure. Together they walked down to the vacant lot and examined the place where Ramrod had been found. Knut grew very excited when they found an enormous sharp stone just where they expected they might. And when they found footprints in the loose clay, bushes that had been trampled down, and finally, to top it all, the unmistakable tire prints of an automobile that had been driven in, had backed up and waited there among the apple trees, he could scarcely contain himself.

But Michael, whose instinct for detective work was usually so easily awakened, remained noticeably unimpressed by the whole business.

Michael had troubles.

His mother's prophecies had come true. And is there anything in the world more irritating to a fourteen-year-old boy than to have to admit that his mother has been right?

Mrs. Wik had spent the whole first period that day telling the class the sad results of their dreaded mid-term examinations.

Michael had been informed that he was failing in both English and mathematics. Math! His best subject! Up to this time he had always been able to take home the glad news that he had made the honor roll in math!

Quite unexpectedly, and all of a sudden, the future looked very bleak. Naturally this would be interpreted at home to mean that his job at the lumberyard was the cause of his bad grades in school. It might even happen that they would make him quit his job. And that would be the everlasting end of his beautiful dream of the motor scooter, the very thought of which had carried Michael through the darkening days of the late autumn and the endless, difficult assignments in school.

Michael dutifully looked all around the area where the accident had happened and listened somewhat absent-mindedly to Knut's scientific interpretation of the conclusions that he felt had to be drawn from the car tracks in the wild, overgrown orchard.

"There have been murderers in this area . . ." Knut said as he got down on all fours.

"Murderers! What kind of nonsense are you talking?" said Michael. He was definitely in a bad mood.

"Murderers . . . well . . ." Knut rose to his feet and made a pretense of brushing off his wrinkled slacks. He realized that he had perhaps exaggerated a bit and, by way of making up for this lapse on his part, decided to show some interest in Michael's troubles.

"How many subjects are you down in anyway?" he asked in a hushed voice as they took the shortest way back to school. It led them straight up a steep, grass-covered precipice, where the frost from the night before still lay— a grim prediction of the darker days to come.

"English and math!" was Michael's quick answer. "And now you can be sure I'll hear 'I told you so' at home."

"Oh, sure, the job. That's too bad, of course. Do you really think that the job is the cause of it all?"

"I wish it were as easy to explain as that! Look, I've studied just as hard as always—even more for that matter. But I got behind way back last fall. I simply can't understand the teacher's explanations in math class—and even when I think I understand, I find that when I get home and start to do my homework, I've forgotten."

"Gee," said Knut comfortingly. "I know exactly what you mean! It isn't the job. I have the same trouble, you know. The truth is, Michael, that there's so darned much confusion in the classroom these days that nobody can learn anything. And the teachers get so mad that they hardly know what they're talking about themselves. I didn't actually fail anything myself, but I had a couple of close calls!"

Michael looked somewhat consoled. A small smile appeared on his face.

"Listen, Knut. Almost everyone in the class failed in one or two—or even three—subjects."

"Three! Don't give me that stuff. That black-haired witch—she's the one who's causing all the commotion in the class if you'll just think about it for a minute—Mary Beth, I mean—she failed in five! Five! And she got bad marks in conduct to boot!"

Because the path was so steep, they stopped to rest for a minute.

They could see their breath as they stood there. Their hands were stiff with cold; they stuck them in their pockets.

"Oh, I think she's kind of fun. Of course, she puts on quite a show!"

Knut gave Michael a quick but searching look.

"That girl is a catastrophe, let me tell you. She is dragging the whole class down. Everybody spends their time staring at her instead of at the blackboard! No, thanks. I can name a good many girls who are worth twenty of her."

All of a sudden Michael became so suspicious of the fact that Knut, the scientist of the class, was talking about "worthwhile girls" that he forgot all about his troubles.

"What do you mean? *Who* do you mean?"

"Well, take Cecilia for example." Knut poked around in a pile of frostbitten leaves with his broad-toed shoe. He didn't manage to sound completely nonchalant; he couldn't hold back his enthusiasm. "You should have seen her last night! She was so sweet about taking care of Ramrod, and she didn't once lose her temper in spite of the fact that I woke her up in the middle of the night."

"Cecilia is a fine girl. Nice. One of the best."

To his own surprise, Michael could hear the strain in his own voice. He found it hard to get the words out. It had something to do with the fact that he could picture in his mind the kitchen in the Acker home at midnight, Cecilia's hair shining in the lamplight, her wonderful way of listening so eagerly . . .

And to think that it was Knut she was listening to instead of to him, Michael.

Suddenly he felt, even more strongly than when Mrs. Wik, in a very chilly voice, told the class what their fate had been, that the whole autumn had been an unlucky one—a dark, dismal period of time with absolutely no highlights.

"The bell's just about to ring," he said briskly. "We've got to hurry!"

Knut looked at him in bewilderment as they ran at full speed across the playground. What thanks was he getting for trying to perk up Michael's morale!

A mood of deepest gloom had settled on Class 4C and stayed there the remainder of the morning. Even though the classroom had been well aired during recess—so much so that the pupils still shivered from the cold—everyone was irritable. With half an ear, Michael heard Knut ask Cecilia to come along with him when he took Ramrod to the veterinarian in the afternoon. To Knut's delight, she answered in the affirmative.

Michael thought that Cecilia, who had managed to escape without any bad grades, looked maddeningly happy and calm. He felt alone, unhappy, and left out, an experience that, in the face of his usually great popularity, he had never had before. However, since in addition he had a pretty fair amount of pride, he made an attempt to hide this strange new feeling of emptiness within himself with a nonchalant attitude, a certain boldness, uncalled-for laughter, and a number of sarcastic remarks. More than one teacher that morning made a mental note that Michael Olmstedt seemed to be developing some highly unexpected and noticeably unpleasant manners.

When the bell rang for lunch, Michael closed his briefcase and rushed out of the classroom without saying a word to anyone. But he hadn't even gotten halfway down the stairs before he heard someone call out his name.

"Michael, wait! We can walk together."

It was Mary Beth. In a twinkling she had caught up with him. Michael slowed down.

"You're always in such a terrible hurry in the afternoons that no one ever gets a chance to have a word with you. Now, at least, you aren't on your way to some stupid old job. What's the matter with you anyway? You seem depressed!"

Mary Beth had appeared at just the right moment. Michael felt that here, at last, was someone friendly—someone whose interest in him was beyond the call of duty. He looked approvingly at her blue-black curly hair. She seemed to carry with her a radiant, almost tropical warmth, which was exceptionally effective on a forbidding, frosty morning such as this one had been.

"Well, I certainly don't have much to be joyful about," he said in an attempt to appear both highly masculine and utterly unconcerned. "Failed in English and math, as you know. And one thing and another."

He suddenly remembered that Mary Beth was much worse off than he was, and he gave her a patronizing but admiring look out of the corner of his eye.

"I don't know how you manage to keep looking this way yourself. You have a few troubles, too, haven't you?"

"Looking what way?" Mary Beth asked in her usual surprised manner—a manner that fooled none of the girls but that none of the boys seemed to be able to see through.

Michael wasn't bewitched by her to the extent that he would let himself be tricked into giving her an old-fashioned compliment, but he looked at the girl beside him with obvious approval and said, "As if you couldn't care less. You seem so utterly unconcerned, I mean. Even after you've found out your grades, and after Mrs. Wik gave you such a bawling out, and everything else!"

Mary Beth shrugged her shoulders as she watched Michael politely taking her turquoise-colored bicycle out of its place in the rack.

"It doesn't bother me a bit! There are a whole lot of other things that are exciting and fun. Why should I give a hang about school?"

Side by side, they bicycled down to the road.

"But what about your parents?" Michael asked. "Don't they say anything if you come home with bad grades?"

"Nah!"

That one little word expressed Mary Beth's whole attitude toward parental authority. She said nothing more.

"Well, it's really disastrous for me," Michael said. Already his problems seemed easier to bear, and he suddenly felt a great desire to entrust himself to Mary Beth's care—a fact that, when he recalled the conversation long afterwards, gave him quite a shock.

"As you know, I work most afternoons. I've been doing it to save money enough to buy a motor scooter, but now probably I won't be allowed to keep the job because of my grades."

"You mean you're working to earn *money?*" At this point Mary Beth's voice came out in a surprising falsetto, but she quickly regained her composure. "I think that's pretty wonderful. Now of course I understand. Failing in English and math is really the living end. . . . But look. Don't be worried about the motor scooter. I have two of them at home, and you can borrow one of them any time you please—if you want to."

"Two!" said Michael. Now it was his turn to speak in a falsetto.

"My brother Peter's old one—he doesn't use it any more —and then my own." Mary Beth had a rather unusual—and enviable—way of managing not to sound boastful. Even now her offhand manner suggested that owning two motor scooters was the most natural thing in the world. It was as if she felt this to be an inalienable right of every single person from birth.

67

Actually, Michael wouldn't have been able to react to any degree even if she had bragged obviously. He was impressed solely by his mental picture of the motor scooter.

"But you aren't fifteen yet, are you?"

"Oh, well, I'll be fifteen in just a few months. And all last summer, you know, I rode around in the country. It was absolutely glorious. Nobody said anything about it. But here in old Nordvik, where every man, woman, and child knows who you are and how old you are, I'd never be able to get away with it. Not in daylight, at least."

Her usually smooth, seductive voice changed into a small laugh.

"But when it's dark? . . ." Involuntarily Michael began to breathe faster.

"Well, you see, sometimes in the evening I go out and practice. That's really none of anyone else's business, do you think? And besides, I have all the proper lights and reflectors, so the snoops really don't have anything to say when they see the scooter. Don't you think it would be fun if we could practice together some evening? Peter's scooter is in fine shape, and you could use it if you wanted. He never uses it because now he has the most powerful motorcycle you can buy."

Michael was unaware of the fact that he had accompanied Mary Beth clear up to her own gate. Neither had he noticed that his good friends, the police, had been spoken of with obvious contempt, nor that the word "snoops" wasn't one commonly used around Nordvik. It could be that a faint echo remained, but if so, it was deep down in his subconscious. The only feeble objection he raised was offset by the eagerness in his voice.

"But, Mary Beth, I don't know how to handle a scooter."

"Look, you can learn all that in ten minutes. There's absolutely nothing to it."

A good deal of Mary Beth's great attraction lay in her way of hastily, shyly withdrawing when she had made a conquest. Right now she had made a conquest, which she followed up with an unobtrusive movement of one hand.

"Look, Michael. Come over to my house this evening. I'll show you the motor scooter, and if you want to, you can try it out."

She disappeared down the birch-lined walk that led up to the Evander house. In conjunction with the white trunks of the birches, her bright green dress seemed to speak of spring.

Michael turned his bicycle around. The frostbitten leaves along the road rustled as he rode through them. He stared straight up in the air, unconscious of the cold, of his bad grades, of everything but the fact that tonight, at last, he could climb on a real motor scooter.

In all honesty, he was even unconscious of the fact that a girl in a duffel coat, a pony tail adorning her stubborn head, bicycled past him and gave him a withering look. In something resembling a complete frenzy, her long legs pedaled wildly.

The girl was Ann Acker, and long before the bell rang for first period after lunch, every single girl in class 4C, and most of the girls in all the other classes, knew that

MADCAP MYSTERY

Michael Olmstedt had walked Mary Beth Evander clear up to her gate.

Michael was having his first brush with one of Nordvik's strictest laws—the absolute impossibility, be it night or day, winter or summer, of taking a girl home without having the news get around.

7

MICHAEL IN FOREIGN TERRITORY

The day, which began with a clear, frosty morning, continued to be icy, though blessed by sunshine and blue skies; toward evening the clouds began to appear. The populace of Nordvik, where the forces of nature seemed to gather themselves closely around every house and to whip through every street of the town, shuddered.

In spite of the fact that the heat had been turned on and the houses were, consequently, quite cozy, such an early display of the winter's might was a grave reality that caused people to shiver at the thought of what was yet to come.

From the attic Michael had gotten down last year's quilted wind-proof jacket and a worn-out ski cap. To his astonishment, he discovered that the distance between where the sleeves of his jacket left off and his hands began was almost four inches. This would hardly do. It certainly didn't add much to his appearance. For a moment he stood there, uncertain. He then decided to hide the unattractive jacket sleeves with a pair of overly long gloves that, admittedly, had seen better days.

With mixed emotions of both hopefulness and doubt, he wondered, as he plodded along the road to Mary Beth's house, whether even she *really* had any desire to be out on a night such as this.

His hopes soared as he stood face to face with Mary Beth in the vestibule of her elegant home. She was dressed in a cherry-red ski jacket, tight-fitting tan pants, and the ubiquitous high boots, which not so long ago had annoyed their teacher, Mrs. Wik, beyond measure. The hood of her jacket was lined with a deep-piled bluish-gray sheepskin, which framed her soft olive-complexioned face very attractively.

Michael was out to have fun—honest-to-goodness masculine sport—and this little touch of luxury was over and above what he had expected—indeed, what he had even wanted. Confused, he stood there blinking his eyes in the face of the powerful electric light that shone from the hall and that seemed even more powerful as it was reflected by three enormous mirrors.

But Mary Beth was poise personified. She said "Hi," to him, and, "We'll go directly to the garage," and not much of anything else.

Michael looked around while she silently put on a pair of fur-lined leather gloves.

"Nice clothes you have!" he remarked with obvious

admiration.

"Do you think so? These gloves are good because they're big and roomy, and they keep your fingers much warmer. I notice the cold most on my fingers and my toes. . . . Peter!" she called out toward a row of rooms that lay plunged in darkness with the exception of a small beam of light at the far end of the corridor. "Peter, we're going down to the garage now."

"Peter's coming along with us tonight," she added as she walked, with squeaking boots, toward the door with Michael close behind her. "I think he has something up his sleeve that might be fun."

"But I didn't have in mind to ride—really ride—out on any road exactly," Michael broke in. His hesitation at this point was for a totally different reason than before.

Mary Beth glanced at him searchingly. Michael was half a head taller than she was, wiry, and in excellent physical condition. She was interested in him for his own sake but, in addition, interested in his appearance. This she managed to hide, however, as she hid nearly everything else, beneath an attitude of total unconcern.

"But of course you're going to ride. I tell you, there's nothing to learning how to handle a motor scooter," was all that she answered.

Quietly they crossed the stone terrace that was surrounded by a latticed balustrade and a number of marble statues. If Cecilia had been at Michael's side, they would have had fun joking about certain of the statues, which, in the faint light from the window, bore resemblance to a few of their mutual friends, and perhaps he would have tried to frighten her as they went down the dark path that led to the garage. But with Mary Beth, he knew for certain he was no longer walking in his baby shoes. He had had every intention of asking Mary Beth about a problem in physics that was a part of their assignment for the next day. But he let it go; he was fully aware that Mary Beth had a sense of values very different from his own, and he had no desire to risk having her snort at him contemptuously.

Not a word was spoken until they stood in the garage and Mary Beth had turned on the lights.

At that point, Michael couldn't keep still any longer.

"What a gigantic garage!" he exclaimed. "Just how many cars do you have anyway?"

"Three," said Mary Beth. "There's Papa's Jaguar, and then we have two Volkswagens. That old wreck over there belongs to the gardener. Now and then he drives for my father's company. And back there are the motor scooters and the motorcycle. There's another exit back there, which is very good, you see, because it leads directly out to Ekenase Hill instead of out toward the main road. There's a little hill outside. You can roll the scooter down, and no one up here can hear that you're going out."

"Don't they know at home that you go out riding in the evenings?"

"Good heavens, no! Mother would have a fit on the spot. Look, this is my motor scooter, and that's Peter's old one. You can have it this evening. And it's a first-class job, too, let me tell you. Peter knows a man who works down at

the Nordvik Machine Shop and who has fooled around with it during his spare time. It will go about thirty-five or forty."

Michael stuck his cap under his arm and bent down beside the shiny black motor scooter. He saw at once that this was no ordinary model; it had a good many optional, extra features.

"This is sort of a cross between a motor scooter and a motorcycle. Special speed tires. I don't know how Peter ever managed to get hold of these extra parts with precisely the right dimensions. What a flying trip you can make on this!"

With a grip that showed both great strength and also knowledge, Mary Beth managed to lift the scooter's stand.

"I think they imported these speed tires from Holland. Papa does a lot of business with a rubber company there. Look here now. Here's the starter. And this handle controls the gas. Here is the throttle. And this is your choke. The brakes are located here. Now, let's turn on the lights. Bright . . . and dim!"

Mary Beth accompanied her sharp, explicit instructions with lightning-quick motions of her hands. There was no denying that here was an area that interested her very much, and one in which she was absolutely sure of herself. Her self-confidence, however, wasn't the sort that made everyone around her suffer from an inferiority complex. It was all beyond Michael's wildest expectations. He drank in the instructions with great enthusiasm, and soon he was able to name all the different parts and locate them correctly.

"Good. You're catching on beautifully. Peter told me that the tank is over half full. Now, let me tell you what we're going to do. Let's turn off the headlights and go out with the scooters completely dark. Then there won't be any light to tip off the gardener as we open the garage doors."

Michael, completely carried away by his dream come true, listened with no more than half an ear.

"What would he do if he found out?" he mumbled absent-mindedly.

"I'm not very fond of having anyone spying on me," she answered curtly. She pulled up the hood of her jacket, which had slipped down while they were talking. "And then, we'll roll them down the hill and put the switch at number one until we come to Ekenase Hill. Then we can turn on the lights and practice for a while. Nobody ever comes around down there."

"But how about your brother?" Michael wondered.

If the truth be told, the only disappointment of the evening was the presence of her brother. Naturally he would be quite a worldly-wise fellow on his elegant motorcycle, which Michael had examined in the garage, and it didn't seem like much fun to have your first lesson with him as the audience.

"He'll be along, but it may take a half hour or so. He's waiting for a telephone call. There'll be enough time for us to ride around down there and for you to learn how to handle the thing. Let's go!"

As she uttered the last words, she turned off the lights without waiting for a reply. Michael stood up and, for a couple of minutes, remained there in the darkness. There were some doubts in his mind. He heard the sound of the side door being opened and saw, leading down from the dark garage, an asphalt-covered path.

His face was wet with perspiration. Breathless with anticipation, he gasped as he felt the intense cold from the outside.

"But listen, Mary Beth," he said in a hushed voice.

"Yes, what do you want?"

"Look, I . . . I really don't know. . . . I've never handled one of these before . . ."

"Well, for heaven's sake, you have to begin *sometime!*"

All at once Michael was ashamed of himself for standing there and not saying what he really wanted to say.

"Well, that may be," he replied in a voice so harsh that Mary Beth, who was just leading her scooter out through the door, halted involuntarily. "It doesn't seem very difficult, and I don't imagine that it is. But I'm not fifteen years old yet, you know. . . . I had just thought I might learn to start it and stuff like that. And I even think it would be marvelous to ride around here in the field below the garage. But I certainly don't want to go out on any road!"

"Oh, what difference could that possibly make! You'll be fifteen in just a couple of months, and it's just as well to learn beforehand."

"No, that idea doesn't appeal to me at all. Papa has said so many times that the line has to be drawn some place, and . . ."

There was deep silence in the huge garage.

78

Michael waited for a reply, much as you listen, after you have thrown a rock into a deep well, for the sound of the stone hitting the bottom. Actually, what he had said could apply equally well to Mary Beth. Would she be angry?

Mary Beth was surprised and, moreover, for once, utterly unsure of herself. She had a scornful answer on the tip of her tongue, but she tried, in vain, to search the darkness and find out what sort of expression Michael had on his face. She hadn't expected that he would raise any objections. She wasn't used to objections.

There was more than a hint of stubbornness in his changing adolescent voice. It demanded a measure of caution. In all truth, Mary Beth thought Michael was very good-looking, and she knew that you had to pay a price now and then to have a good-looking boy friend.

"Well," she said calculatedly, "if that's the way you feel about it, I guess. . . . But down there in the field we can't get into any trouble. You can walk down with your scooter, and I'll ride down ahead to Ekenase Hill. There aren't any roads near there, and we can stay pretty close to the slope. The ground is good and solid, and you can start and stop wherever you please. So, let's go. See you in a few minutes."

Michael watched the huge shapeless silhouette of the girl and the scooter as they disappeared down the path. He heard the sound of the gravel under the wheels as she rolled down the slope and the sound of the motor as she started it farther down. After a couple of unsuccessful attempts, he finally got his own machine in gear and slowly followed along.

Ekenase Hill was a stony promontory that projected out into Nordvik Bay. For years it had been the subject of many a discussion among the city fathers, especially those on the Zoning Commission. Because of its marvelous location, halfway between the sweep of the sea and the rolling meadows along the shore, many people had seen the possibilities of developing the area into something that, so they declared, would greatly benefit the citizenry of Nordvik. Applications had flooded the Zoning Commission's office, offering to finance dance restaurants, theaters, or beach resorts.

In reality, the hill offered little more than stones, low, scrubby bushes, wild blueberries, and heather at water level; the beach was shallow. But it had its virtues. During the daytime it served as a favorite playground for little children, and in the evenings, when the moonlight skimmed along the tops of the waves, as a promenade for young couples.

As Mary Beth had promised, Michael found her on the grassy hill leading down to the shore. The lights on her scooter were on, and the motor was idling.

"The ground is solid here, and it's not muddy," she said calmly. "We can ride around here."

Apparently she had forgotten the recent exchange of words.

"You look cute," he called out above the noise of the motor. "Just like a little imp."

For a while they rode around in circles or figure-eights, sometimes one after the other, sometimes in different directions.

Mary Beth suggested that they might play follow-the-leader on the small paths between the heather and the stones just a little way up the hill, and this turned out to be a good idea. They made all kinds of turns, rode over all manner of ruts, and, in general, performed some pretty fair maneuvers.

Michael was having a great time. With every moment he felt his ability to handle the machine, which at the beginning seemed unexpectedly cumbersome, growing better and better. Just imagine. One of these days he would have a motor scooter of his own and could ride around all over Nordvik, or wherever he pleased. He would take Cecilia for a ride. . . . Oh, and Mary Beth, too, but of course she already had one of her own. . . .

Forgotten were the bad grades, and the physics problems; forgotten was the whole world except for the circle of light issuing from the front of the scooter. . . .

All of a sudden Mary Beth put on her brakes so violently and so unexpectedly that Michael had to veer off to the side to avoid hitting her.

"They're coming now," she said as she stood listening in the direction of the road above. She shut off her motor and put the hood of her jacket down in order to be able to hear better. "Yes, I'm sure of it."

Michael, too, turned off his motor.

He noticed the change in her tone of voice and suddenly sensed that her whole attitude toward their game had been one of utter apathy—out-and-out indifference.

"What do you mean by 'they'?" he asked.

"Peter. Peter and . . . well, he has a couple of pals he

chums around with. They're all crazy about motorcycles—every last one of them. I'm going to ride up and meet them!"

She started her motor and took off over the stony, deeply-rutted ground with such speed and boldness that Michael realized all too well that their follow-the-leader had been, for her, a childish game—a childish game planned on his behalf.

The earth-shaking noise of several motorcycles finally died down as they slackened their speed. Michael, who had been none too happy at having been left down by the shore, could make out several voices, among them Mary Beth's. But the whole time the motors sounded impatiently in the background. Halfheartedly, Michael made an unsuccessful attempt to start the motor of his machine again. He had the overwhelming feeling that he was a fifth wheel. His cheeks seemed to be on fire. . . . Why had Mary Beth invited him over if, all the while, she would really rather have rushed off on the open road with Peter and his gang? Certainly, it had been fun to try out a motor scooter, but Michael had, at length, realized that it would really only be fun when he had his own to fool around with.

The longer the discussion continued up there, the more uncomfortable he felt. When Mary Beth finally returned, he had decided to thank her for giving him a lesson and to take off for home.

"Listen, Michael," said Mary Beth breathlessly, "you see, Peter and the other guys have something planned that sounds like a ball. The plan is that we're going to ride up towards Lindeby, and then we're all going to have a party in a villa somewhere in that neighborhood. . . ."

She paused to catch her breath, and when she continued, her voice had regained its very special monotonous quality that Michael remembered so well from school.

"Well, I didn't say that very well. What I really meant to say was that we have an aunt and uncle who live there, and they're off on a trip at the moment. They're in Majorca. But we have the key to their house, because they're awfully nice, and they said that if we wanted to have a party while they were away, we could have it there. Mother is always so dead-tired, and she detests it when the boys make a lot of noise. Our aunt and uncle haven't any children of their own, and as a result, they've always been wonderful to Peter and me. Oh, Michael, you can come along, can't you?"

Mary Beth's voice sounded unusually imploring. At this point it was Michael's turn to try to see the expression on *her* face. It wasn't at all like her to plead or even to let herself in for much of anything at all. He hesitated.

"We can leave the scooters here and ride behind the fellows," she added hastily.

Michael knew full well what she really wanted to say. She didn't want to provide an opportunity for the others to make fun of him simply because he refused to ride a scooter before he was fifteen. She was so desperately anxious to go along herself that she didn't even mind if she couldn't ride her own scooter.

Actually, she had been very nice to him the whole evening!

"O.K.," he said briskly. "If they want us to come along, O.K. We can come back here on the way home and get the scooters."

The boys waiting up there on the hill could no longer conceal their impatience. With their motors emitting a deafening roar, they rode in circles, one after the other. Michael could see that there were four of them. And all four looked exactly alike, dressed in the mandatory outfit —a white crash helmet, a black leather jacket, and goggles. He couldn't make out their facial features, but the one who first got off his motorcycle and came over toward them was clearly Mary Beth's brother.

"Oh, so you finally came," was all that he said. "Now, let's get going. Fighter!" he shouted to one of the others. "You take my sister behind you!"

Michael understood immediately that these were motorcycle enthusiasts of the first order, whose reigning god was speed. Without a word he climbed onto the back of Peter's motorcycle.

Without losing a minute's time, Peter accelerated the powerful machine with a deafening noise. With Peter as the leader, the group sped through the silent, dark streets of the town.

8

BLOCKADE

Lindeby was about three miles up the coast. The small houses, the modern stores, the residential area with its many apartment houses spoke eloquently of the fact that it was a much younger suburb than Nordvik. It could boast of an elegant supper club with a dance floor but with none too spotless a reputation, an ultra-modern movie house with an intimate, fully-equipped soda fountain on the side, and a newly constructed school, which, at a distance, looked as if three quarters of it had been built out of glass.

Michael knew that it was not uncommon among certain groups in Nordvik to look upon their own home town as hopelessly conservative and behind the times. To them, Lindeby was the very model of progress. They spent almost all of their free hours there. As for Michael, he had never been there before.

The dark autumn evening was, for him, mainly a bewildering potpourri of neon lights, unfinished houses or newly dug excavations, and a paved superhighway, which, from the point of view of speed alone, cast an intoxicating influence over Peter and his friends. The superhighway followed the coast for over half a mile, and the traffic was heavy. Michael soon realized that his old ski cap wasn't much of a shield against the wind, especially at the speed they were going. He hunched himself up in back of Peter and held fast to Peter's wide safety belt.

When they had gotten about halfway up the highway, it happened. Because of his hunched position, Michael hadn't noticed anything up to the time he heard Peter swear under his breath and felt that the speed had been appreciably slackened. When he looked over Peter's broad shoulders, he knew immediately what had happened, because the whole roadway was brilliantly lighted by a row of revolving lights placed tightly in a row.

Several vehicles had stopped at the side of the road, and all around them could be seen a number of towering figures in black uniforms, with flashing buttons on their shoulder flaps. One of them stepped out into the roadway right in front of Peter's motorcycle. Above his head he held a sign that said "State Police."

Peter put on the brakes and stopped. The motorcycle back of them on which Mary Beth was riding rolled to a stop alongside them. The driver, the one they had called "Fighter," leaned over toward Peter. He said something that Michael was unable to hear. Peter answered with a new swear word. Then Fighter spoke a good deal louder, but whether from excitement or in an attempt to make himself heard above the noise of the motors Michael had no idea.

"Let's get out of here!"

"You idiot!" Peter nearly shouted.

Michael silently agreed with Peter. On the side of the road were a number of police motorcycles, ready to take off at a moment's notice if necessary. There wasn't a chance in the world to clear out of there, and why would he even suggest something so stupid? Insofar as Michael could tell, Peter and all his friends had the necessary equipment on their motorcycles, and all the machines were in good condition.

While Peter and Fighter were agitatedly exchanging comments, one of the officers had reached the place where they had stopped. He stood right beside Michael. He was a tall, powerful man with a pleasant but commanding voice.

"State Police Traffic Command," he said as he continued to circle their group. "We're having a road check here. We'll be back as soon as it's your turn. There are a couple of cars in line before you."

With brisk steps he went on his way. Peter cut the motor, and the others followed his example. All at once it became so astonishingly quiet that you could hear the voices of the policemen and the strange—strange, at least under the circumstances—sound of the lapping of the waves against the rocks on shore.

No one in the group said a word for a long while. The one who finally broke the silence was Mary Beth.

"It's a good thing that I'm not riding on my own motor scooter right now," she said in a low voice. "They would have arrested me for sure because I'm not fifteen yet. Michael, I have you to thank for that."

Before Michael could answer, Peter turned with a jerk toward his sister.

"Thank!" he hissed. "It's the two of you we have to thank that we're sitting here right now. If we hadn't had to wait so long for you, we could have passed this point a long time ago."

Michael loosened his grip on Peter's belt. In the confusion he had continued to hold on for all he was worth. Now a feeling of intense discomfort flowed through his whole body. Yes, it was just as he had suspected. Mary Beth had had to talk them into letting him come along. Even the roots of his hair felt uncomfortably hot.

"Look, I'd just as soon get off right here on the spot," he said impetuously. "I . . ." Search as he might, no words came.

Mary Beth reached out her hand and touched him on the arm.

"Don't pay any attention to him," she said almost pleadingly. There was a little quiver in her voice that somehow stifled Michael's anger more than had her words themselves.

Again everything was quiet. The silence seemed to give vent to all their unexpressed feelings.

Michael took a good look at the situation. In some

strange way the words that had been exchanged had awakened his critical, alert sensitivities.

Fighter had pushed both his helmet and his goggles up and away from his face. Michael stared at him. The whole effect was disappointing; the face that had been concealed by all the equipment resembled that of a fox, with a sharp nose, freckled complexion, and sandy-colored hair peeping down over his forehead. No longer did he look very self-assured. Michael wondered how much of Fighter's hard-boiled appearance depended upon his equipment. To judge from his suggestion, "Let's get out of here," it was apparently a considerable per cent.

One of the cars that had been stopped suddenly started. One of the constables motioned to the motorcycle group to come forward. The spot check seemed to be over.

Two policemen came up to Peter and Michael. The older of the two began to talk. The younger looked at the license plate and began to make notations in his book.

"This is a routine check. May I see your driver's license?"

"Yes, here it is."

"Thank you. Seems O.K. What about your name plate and your tax stamp? Oh, yes. I see it right here. And you are coming from . . . ?"

"Nordvik."

Peter replied hastily and not without some gruffness. Michael, who with admiration had noticed the skilled, firm, and yet agreeable manner in which the policemen performed their duties, suddenly felt embarrassed and turned his face in the opposite direction. Why was Peter speaking this way? The policemen were only doing their duty, even if Peter's papers were all in order.

The policemen's manners continued unchanged. It was possible that his voice was just a bit more authoritative than it had previously been.

"And your destination?"

For the first time, Michael noticed that in the bright lights every change of expression on Peter's face—even *he* had removed his goggles—was unpleasantly highlighted.

It was quite clear that Peter hadn't expected this last question. Up to this moment, his answers had been so prompt that now a delay of even a second or two became noticeable.

"We're just out . . . riding around for fun."

For a moment or so the constable focused his attention on Michael's face. Michael blushed. He knew that he looked startled.

"Uh huh! Riding around for fun, huh! Are all these motorcyclists together?"

"Yeah."

"Hmmm. Four. Let's see about your reflectors."

He addressed these words to the younger constable.

"The lights are all in order. Let me see your dims. This is a powerful machine you have."

Suddenly, unexpectedly, he turned to Michael.

"And your name?"

Michael was so taken by surprise that he actually stammered over the first syllable.

"Mi . . . Michael Olmstedt."

"Are all of you from Nordvik?"

"I . . . I . . . think so."

Peter gave Michael an inexplicably furious look.

"Shut up," he said. "I'll do the talking."

"Yes," he said to the constable.

With great care the constable observed them all—Fighter, Mary Beth, and the others.

He signaled to a group of policemen who were standing a little distance down the road. Briskly one of them walked up into the light. To his immeasurable consternation, Michael recognized him—Inspector Nilsson of the Nordvik Police.

The consternation, Michael noticed at once, began to change into a feeling of intensely unpleasant proportions. Peter. Mary Beth. Fighter. Wouldn't the inspector be surprised! Funny, isn't it, what mental images crop up to haunt you now and then—images that cruelly but effectively manage to lay bare your entire soul. The picture of three faces suddenly appeared in his subconscious mind: Knut . . . Cecilia . . . Carl Axel.

Indeed, the inspector *was* surprised. His small, narrow, icy blue eyes glanced sharply at Peter. And when he saw who was right behind Peter, he stopped dead in his tracks.

"Mi-i-chael!"

Michael made an enormous effort to bow to the inspector.

"Good evening . . . Inspector Nilsson!"

"Well, well, well. You're out on a joy ride. Pretty cold this evening, isn't it?"

The constable—the one who had first interrogated Peter—looked somewhat bewildered.

"I thought since this whole group was from Nordvik that you'd be interested."

"And I am interested. This boy is one of my spies." The inspector's voice was warm and jovial, but Michael noticed that he wasn't missing a single detail of either the group or their motorcycles. Completely unexpectedly, he stretched out his huge gloved hand toward Peter.

"Nilsson," he said. "Nilsson of Nordvik's police."

"Evander!" answered Peter curtly.

"Evander? Oh, yes, of course. Evander." Inspector Nilsson seemed to think all was well. He turned to his colleague.

"Is everything O.K.? Well, on your way."

Both of them saluted.

"It doesn't matter to us if we have to turn around here. We're just out riding for the fun of it," Peter said.

"Home," he shouted to Fighter, who was once again hiding under his helmet. Michael noticed the surprised expression on Mary Beth's face. Peter kicked at the starter frenetically . . . once . . . twice. Finally the motor started.

But in the few seconds before all other sounds were drowned out, Michael heard these words that Peter hissed over his shoulder:

"So, I guess you know everybody in town, huh?"

BLOCKADE

9

LITTLE PITCHERS

"That Michael!" said Erik Acker as he poured sugar on his cereal, covering it thoroughly. "That Michael—the one you like so much, Cecie—he was out with that girl named Beth yesterday evening. And with a whole gang of motorcycle hoods. Thieves. All of them!"

Spoons dropped. Glasses were put down. Around the breakfast table, the whole family stopped chewing.

"What did I tell you?" Ann remarked.

"What's Erik babbling about?" asked Mrs. Acker.

"Oh, he's just making up things, as usual," Cecilia replied.

Erik continued to put sugar on his cereal. He loved to gossip.

"Well," he declared, "if they weren't thieves, at least

94

they were chiddnapers. They chiddnaped Michael!"

"Nobody in the world could chiddnap Michael against his wishes, you silly goof," Cecilia said with a superior air. "And, another thing. The word is kidnap, not chiddnap. So there!"

"What did the hoods look like?" Ann asked amiably. She was afraid that Erik might have been so insulted that he wouldn't want to finish the whole story.

"There's only one way for hoods to look," said Erik, amazed at such gross ignorance. He squinted at his cereal dish to check and see that it was sufficiently covered with sugar. "Michael and that Beth, or whatever her name is, were down riding motor scooters on Ekenase Hill all of yesterday evening!"

"And how do you know?" Mrs. Acker asked.

"Well, I was just going to tell you," Erik explained as he resumed the sugaring operation. "Me and Johnnie were down there trying to get Kat out of the tree. Some old dog had chased him up, and he didn't have the nerve to come down all by himself. Instead he sat there crying, and then he climbed up farther."

"But, Erik! You aren't allowed to go down to the shore that late at night. Ann, why didn't you forbid him to go?"

Ann, who had been the baby sitter the previous evening, immediately attacked her little brother.

"What are you talking about? You know good and well that you weren't out yesterday evening!"

"Oh, I wasn't, wasn't I? Do you think you know everything that goes on in this world?" Erik yelled indignantly as he spilled sugar all over the plate and the tablecloth. It was very seldom that no one paid the slightest attention to how much sugar he used. "I sneaked out the kitchen door after you thought I'd gone to bed!"

The youngest member of the Acker family, who suddenly discovered that his feeding spoon was no longer coming to his mouth at regular intervals, stood the situation, with wide-open mouth, for a few seconds before letting out a horrifying shriek.

Quickly Mrs. Acker filled the spoon and gave it to him.

"Did you get the cat down?" Cecilia asked. At this point it was she who wanted to calm Erik down.

"We took a sardine and a rake with us," he said with his mouth full of cereal. "After hours and hours he came down. But I can tell you, we had a ball watching that guy Michael and that dish he was with."

"Didn't they see you?"

"Nah. We were just as quiet as mice," Erik said as he began again to sugar his cereal. "And then the hoods arrived. The black-haired dish said"—Erik put his head to the side and imitated Mary Beth's voice—" 'Oh, Michael, you can come along, can't you?' "

Dead silence reigned around the breakfast table at the Acker house. At that point, Henrik, who had been silently enjoying the entertaining description, broke out in a gale of laughter.

Erik looked highly pleased with himself. He was clearly at his best with an appreciative public.

"Yes, and boy, oh boy, were they ever silly!" he remarked in his best grown-up fashion. "You should have seen him. He thought he could handle a motor scooter! This was what he was doing . . . !"

With imaginary handle bars, Erik demonstrated Michael's awkwardness. Unfortunately, he managed to knock over the sugar bowl.

"Oh, well. There wasn't much in it anyway," he announced reassuringly as he picked it up.

"Erik, you quiet down right this minute and eat up your cereal! Ann, put the sugar bowl away." Mrs. Acker turned to Cecilia. "That Evander girl—isn't she a good deal older than the others in your class?"

"No, I don't think so," Cecilia answered, noticeably calmer. "Six months at the very most. She failed five subjects and got terrible marks in conduct, too, at mid-term. Listen, Erik, those hoods they were with must have been Peter Evander and his gang. And they're not any gang of thieves, let me tell you. You talk so much nonsense you drive me out of my mind!"

"Well, they *looked* like thieves," Erik persisted stubbornly. He didn't, however, continue to expound his views on the subject but instead devoted his efforts to his cereal.

Suddenly Cecilia pushed her cup of hot chocolate away.

"May I leave the table?" she asked. "I have to study my physics lesson."

At once her mother looked up. She opened her mouth to comment dutifully, "You haven't eaten anything," but she stopped herself. There was something strange about

Cecilia's voice these days. Lately Mrs. Acker had begun to be very sensitive to these subtle changes.

"Go ahead and study, dear," she said calmly. "Here, Mr. Primeval Brat! Here comes the last spoonful."

10

THE SNOWMAN

After several nights of frost, clouds suddenly appeared in the northeast and it began to snow. At first the snow was accompanied by strong winds from the sea. The wind, however, soon subsided, but the snow seemed determined to demonstrate that it could handle itself even without the wind's help. It fell and fell obstinately, covering the meadows along the shore and the piers, where a few motorboats, not yet put away for the winter, remained moored, and the gardens and the orchards, where there were quantities of foods that had not yet been gathered and stored for the winter.

"The first snow is awfully early this year," the people of Nordvik commented to one another. "Nobody has had time to replant the flower bulbs yet. But that doesn't matter. This snow will never last!"

Little did they know.

The snow and the mercury were plotting a conspiracy. The temperature fell to 40°, to 35°, and finally to 22°.

The bay froze over. The last leaves, which had been badly beaten by the northeaster, gave up the battle. In the space of a single night the trees were transformed into blackened, praying arms outstretched toward an uncompromising sky. In a few short hours the beach toys, which only a little while before had looked so inviting and appropriate in the soft sand, became immovable and buried once and for all by piles of snow. In just one night, the snowdrifts clogged the roads and streets.

The snowplows—pitifully few of them—wakened with a start from their summer nap and were put to work. Abandoned automobiles lined all the thoroughfares. Tow trucks and emergency vehicles were on duty night and day.

Finally the last fortress collapsed. The students, usually persistent beyond any reasonable degree, were forced to put away their bicycles and to walk to school.

"Well, if this isn't the end! Having to *walk* to school in October!" said Knut, his voice half smothered by his heaviest, longest scarf, which seemed to be wound, in boa-constrictor fashion, around the whole upper half of his body. Trying to hurry because they were late, he and Michael, as well as about 80 per cent of the school population, struggled up the hill leading to the school building. Though half blinded by snow, they managed finally to reach the playground, and they nodded good-morning greetings to Cecilia and Ulla. At that moment, a shiny black Jaguar, which stirred up a cloud of snow as it went, drove up right in front of the steps.

Out of the car jumped Mary Beth in her red jacket, followed by her brother Peter, dressed in white from head to foot.

Ulla glanced at them sharply.

"Those white jackets are apparently high fashion in the winter sports centers in Switzerland," she managed to blurt out as she struggled to pull her leg out of a snowdrift that was knee high. "I saw in the paper that it's even going to be the latest thing here, too. What do you think of them?"

Knut stuck the tip of his nose out of the scarf and took a good look at them as they disappeared through the entrance door.

"Too feminine for me," he commented ungraciously.

Michael kept still.

"Well, I think it's at least nicer than his old leather jacket and those motorcycle clothes," said Cecilia as she gave Michael a pointedly withering look.

The bell rang. They had to hurry up the steps.

In the corridor outside 4C's home room, Mary Beth was combing her shiny black hair and pressing it into nice waves with her nimble fingers.

"Hi there," she said. Glancing obliquely over her shoulder, she smiled at Michael, and at him alone. "You look like a blizzard has just hit you!"

Michael didn't answer. Loudly he stamped his feet to get the snow off his boots; he began to remove his jacket.

Mary Beth leaned against the wall alongside him. She

had on a heavy cream-colored sweater, and in spite of the fact that it was at least two sizes too big for her—this was the way all the girls wore their sweaters—she managed to look very gracious and to show off her nice figure.

"This cold weather is just too much. Listen . . ." she added, lowering her voice and glancing sideways at Cecilia, "they're coming to pick Peter and me up with the car at one o'clock. We'd be glad to drive you home, and that way you wouldn't have to slop through all that snow. You certainly don't work at the lumberyard on Saturdays, do you, even though we have a half day of school?"

Cecilia, who had heard Mary Beth's remarks and didn't wish to hear Michael's answer, hurried past them and went into the classroom. She held her head just a bit higher than usual. For some reason, Michael caught a glimpse of the back of her neck just at that moment. He didn't immediately comment on Mary Beth's suggestion.

All the while, Knut, with a good deal of help from Ulla, had been extricating himself from his scarf. He, too, had heard the question, and he was aware of Michael's hesitation. The whole of his masculine loathing of domineering females came out in full bloom.

"Oh, no," he said in a harsh voice. He wasn't two inches away from Mary Beth's ear. "Michael can't ride home with you because he's going somewhere with me and"—Knut hastily looked all around—"Cecilia and Ulla and Carl Axel! We're all going out and play in the snow. Hurrah for the snow! We're going to build a snowman. Don't you remember, Michael, you dope?"

Michael laughed resoundingly. Mary Beth was a very clinging female. That fact was obvious.

"That's right!" he bellowed. "I'd forgotten all about it, Knut, old boy. Cecilia . . ."

"Quiet down, you guys," Ulla whispered as she stood behind the boys. "Move. Here comes the teacher!"

With the usual barely perceptible smile on her face, Mary Beth went to her desk at the other side of the classroom. She seemed neither angry nor disturbed. But anyone observing her closely might have noticed that several times during the next period she looked in the direction of Cecilia's desk with a contemplative expression in her eyes.

"You're out of your mind!" said Ulla to Knut when the bell had rung after the last period. The classmates gathered up their books. "Build a snowman! Have you gone into your second childhood or something?"

"Haven't gotten out of my first one yet," Knut assured her. "Well, let's go play. Cecilia, you're coming along, aren't you?"

Cecilia nodded and laughed. She had laughed a good many times that morning. Michael, who stood beside her, suddenly noticed that she still had a little of her summer suntan left. It was most noticeable along the hairline, right there by her ear . . .

"I wouldn't mind so much if we could do some skiing!" Ulla grumbled. "But a snowman! And anyway, the snow isn't wet enough!"

"Oh, but it is," said Carl Axel. "It's real snowman snow. It's gotten much warmer outside."

"Yeah, all the way up to 32°!" Knut informed them triumphantly. "Don't give us a bad time, Ulla. Come on!"

"Not on the schoolgrounds," Ulla said emphatically. "We'd look too dopey!"

"Oh, well, if you're so darned embarrassed, I guess we can go to that old vacant lot down below."

Just as they left the building the Evanders' Jaguar made its appearance on the scene.

"There. You see," Knut whispered eagerly. "Look what we saved Michael from. A fate worse than death. The whole business of being swallowed up by the Evander millions. . . . That's why I thought up the idea of the snowman!"

"Oh, so that's what you had in mind." Ulla looked vastly relieved. "That's pretty smart of you, Knut. But now the snowman has served his purpose. Let's all go home."

But the others protested strongly. Cecilia voiced their collective thoughts.

"I've looked forward all day long to the snowman. Let's go."

Teen-age dignity was suddenly forgotten completely. With awkward, almost childish leaps, they made their way down the hill. Snowballs flew wildly through the air. In no time the boys were having a real snowball battle. Meanwhile, the girls found a spot behind the apple trees. The wind had carried most of the snow away around there.

"Here's a good place for him," said Cecilia. "Cut out your fighting, you guys, and give us a hand. The snow is simply marvelous. Just wet enough. It's great!"

"Yes, this is a fine place," Ulla agreed. "And nobody can see us from the road."

The wind had died down completely, and the sun was trying hard to send down a few rosy-colored beams to filter through the treetops. Blackbirds and field mice hopped out from under the tangled thickets, crestfallen at not being able to find a trace of their hastily buried winter provisions. You could hear the pheasants squawking petulantly among the bushes.

"They sound like tired old, old ladies," Carl Axel commented.

"Like old, grouchy men, I think!" Ulla countered promptly.

Carl Axel and Michael were in the process of rolling an enormous ball of snow. This was to be the foundation of the snowman.

Ulla and Cecilia each had a ball under way.

Knut scurried around looking for animal tracks.

"I'm thinking of saving myself for the most important task—the artistic decoration of this sculptural masterpiece!" he announced.

"That's not hard to believe," Ulla muttered. "Trick everybody into a lot of work. That's all you ever do."

"Certainly. Typical action on the part of one who has as much leadership as I!" Knut explained modestly.

The snow, which wasn't very deep where they were—it had been carried off to deeper drifts along a couple of scrubby ridges—began to run out. They had to roll their balls off in another direction and go a little farther away.

There under the trees Cecilia's hair looked almost metal-

lic in the faint sunshine. She had found a small hill. With great energy she rolled her ball up the slope. Being the oldest in her family, she very seldom had time to indulge in games. And another thing—she was somewhat hesitant about behaving in an undignified manner. But now that both Ulla and Michael and the others were along, she was having a marvelous time. She had on her navy-blue ski suit, the only trimming on which was the gray fur on the hood of her jacket. She looked thin and almost childishly young. Rolling her snowball, she disappeared over the top of the little hill.

A pheasant hen's quarrelsome cry was heard. It was even more unpleasant than usual.

More or less as a weak echo of the pheasant, another little cry was heard.

Michael suddenly straightened up. He tried to get his hair out of his eyes by means of a violent jerk of his head.

"Shhhh!" he said. "Did you hear that?"

"The old pheasant? Yes, I heard it," Carl Axel snorted. "It almost blew my ear off."

Knut returned from his search among the bushes. "That last noise was no pheasant," he said. "That was a person who cried out!"

"I thought . . . ." said Michael. He looked all around. "Hey, where's Cecilia?" he asked.

"Cecilia?" said Ulla as she clapped her mittens together to get rid of the snow. "She's right here—or—well, she *was* right beside me just a minute ago. Cecilia! Cecie! Cecilia-a-a-a-a!"

The creaking adolescent voices of the boys joined in

with Ulla's loud, clear call. You could hear the shouts far and wide. Even the pheasants were quiet. Both they and a bunch of smaller birds decided it was a good time to spread their wings and fly off.

"That's peculiar," Ulla remarked. "Where could she have gone? She can't be very far away. It wasn't two minutes ago that . . ."

"Where did you last see her?" Michael interrupted. In just two long steps he had reached Ulla's side.

"Right there! She rolled her ball up that hill right by that stone!"

Before she had finished her sentence, Michael was up the hill. Knut and Carl Axel followed him a little more slowly. Once Michael had really gone into action, he made anyone else look as if he were slow motion personified.

"No sign of her from here!" Carl Axel said from the top of the hill. From their vantage point they could see the whole slope leading up to the school. In the other direction was a hill covered with thickets and old dead branches, which led to a barbed wire fence, which surrounded the brick-red buildings of the lumberyard. You could see the buildings clearly. Cecilia couldn't have gone off in that direction!

Very cautiously, Michael had begun to go down the other side of the hill. Halfway down, he stopped in his tracks. The snow was over his knees. He pointed at something when he heard what Carl Axel had said.

"Do you think she grew wings?" he called up to the others. "Can't you see her footprints? They end right here. Yes, and down there is her snowball!"

They watched him bend forward. He motioned to them.

"Come down here and take a look." Suddenly his voice was hushed and excited. "Come on down, but do it carefully!"

THE SNOWMAN

11

TRACKS IN THE SNOW

"Could she have fallen down with the ball?" Ulla asked. In utter bewilderment all four of them looked at the huge snowball at the foot of the small hill and at the untracked, smooth white snow all around.

"Well, in that case she'd still be lying there," Carl Axel reminded them in a voice that betrayed that he was none too sure of himself.

"Here is her last footprint," Michael pointed out. "No, look. Stand still and don't move around too much and destroy the footprints. That's the only thing we have to go on."

Knut, who had been standing in silence, began to fidget anxiously.

"This is the place where Ramrod got hurt," he said in a hushed voice.

Then everything became quiet. It was a silence that could only exist on a motionless, still winter day when everything in the world seems blanketed by snow.

Ulla's words eased the tension. Until she spoke, they had been on the verge of being terrified.

"Cecilia can't have been hit by anything or anybody. Here it is—the middle of the day. And she was right here so close to all of us," she said. "Maybe she suddenly felt ill and took off for home."

"By helicopter in that case," Knut retorted.

"Now look, we've got to think this out," Michael said, more for his own benefit than for that of his friends. "Here the footprints end. There's the snowball down there. We heard a cry—I can almost swear that it must have been Cecilia who cried—and she doesn't have wings. . . . She must have. . . . Great heavens! Now I know." At once he got down on all fours.

"Well, you might share your secret with us!" Knut suggested.

Michael pulled off his mittens. Slowly he crept around in the snow.

"There must be a hole here," he shouted excitedly. "The snow is so deep that you can't tell where it is, but it must be here somewhere. She must have fallen down through here somewhere!"

"Are you completely out of your mind?" Ulla cried.

Michael began to plow around with his bare hands. Knut and Carl Axel helped him.

"Don't go too close!" Michael warned them. "Creep along on all fours!"

111

He stuck his arm down into the depression in the snow. He turned his face upwards toward his friends. Breathlessly they followed every movement of his face. His whole arm disappeared, clear up to his shoulder.

Ulla's big brown eyes, usually so keen, had clouded up, and she looked terrified.

"But if she's down there, why doesn't she say anything?"

Michael's mouth was turned up at the corners. But none of them mistook his strange expression for a smile. It was a gesture born of excitement and of pure nervousness. He seemed to be listening with both his eyes and his ears.

Suddenly he crouched down and put his face to the hole.

"Cecie," he cried. "Cecilia! Can you hear me? Cecilia-a-a-a!"

The cry seemed to roll under their feet, sounding hollow and echoing as if it had lost itself in some enormous vault under the earth. The sound left no doubt in their minds.

"It's absolutely hollow down there!" Carl Axel commented. "There must be something under us here."

"A cellar of some kind," said Knut. "I'll bet I know what it is. One of those cellars they used to have in the old days. We're standing on the kind of little hill they used to build up around them. The entrance is on the side of the hill, but it's probably overgrown to such an extent that you'd never notice it."

"But are you absolutely sure that Cecie's down there?

112

That she isn't trying to answer you?" Ulla said quakingly. "Try to call down again, Michael."

Michael called out; again the results were negative. Once more he plowed around in the snow where the hole was. Suddenly he stopped and moved his hands more slowly.

"There's something here," he said. "Something hard. Wait. I think I can move it. It seems pretty loose!"

He managed to get a grip on it. He shook. He pulled. From under the snow he pulled out a piece of galvanized sheet metal. Ramrod would have growled; he would have recognized it if he had been around . . .

"Aha!" Michael said. "Now I understand. This piece of sheet metal has been over the hole so that it wouldn't rain or snow down into the cellar. Cecilia was coming down the hill. She must have braced herself so that she wouldn't slide down. I guess the sheet metal moved and Cecilia fell into the hole!"

"Don't talk so darned much," said Knut, who was fond of lecturing others. "If she fell down there, why doesn't she say something?"

"That's just what we have to find out as fast as possible," said Michael. "We can't waste time trying to find the door. I guess I'll have to hop down into the hole. If I disappear too, you'll have to send for help."

As he continued to talk, he began to let himself down into the hole. He hung by his elbows. Only the upper half of his body was visible.

113

"Take it easy," Carl Axel warned him. "The edges you're hanging onto aren't much to depend on!"

"I'll . . . be . . . very careful," he said almost breathlessly. They could see that he was swinging his legs as he hung there.

"I think I'm going to make it," he continued. "There's a shelf or something down here that I think I can stand on, if only it will hold me. . . . Yes, I guess it will hold my weight. Hey, wait a minute! I just thought of something. I think I'll probably need something to give me a little light down there. Have any of you got any matches?"

Knut, whose pockets were always full of one thing and another, took out a package immediately.

"Here you are," he said. "Oh, I forgot. You're without hands! Hold on. I'll put it in your breast pocket."

"Thanks. That will help. Well, so long!"

Slowly Michael's head and shoulders disappeared. The others crept cautiously to the mouth of the hole and tried to look down in.

The foothold that Michael had managed to find in the old cellar evidently held him. But since he didn't know quite what it was or how big it was, he didn't dare move his feet. He curled up like a cat. With careful, beautifully calculated movements, he managed to take Knut's package of matches out of his pocket. He struck one, but it went out almost immediately because of the draft that was coming down from the hole in the roof.

During the split second it was lighted, he managed to discover, to his delight, that he sat curled up on the outside edge of an old cask. Moreover, he got a hasty impression that this was a large, old-fashioned cellar, with shelves all around on which were bottles and boxes. In addition, he caught a glimpse of something that lay on the earthen floor at the foot of the cask. It looked for all the world like a bundle of old clothes, but Michael did see, for one second, something that looked like a lock of blond hair.

Now the voices from above reached him.

"Hey, are you all right down there?"

"Can you see anything?"

Summoning all his powers, Michael managed to make his hands stop shaking; he struck another match.

This time he was more careful; he cupped his hands to shield the light from the draft.

Then he saw the old, familiar navy-blue ski suit, the hood with fur trimming it, and, half hidden under a shelf of some kind, Cecilia's light hair. A table had evidently toppled down; it lay across her legs. Apparently she had dragged it with her as she fell.

The match went out.

Michael realized that the first thing he had to have was better illumination.

"Hey up there," he shouted. "Can you hear me? Fine! She's down here. She must have hit her head. I can't do anything much with just matches."

Outside the hole, Knut, Carl Axel, and Ulla looked at each other in dismay. Knut dug around in his pockets. After a couple of minutes he dragged out a four-inch stump of candle from one of his inside pockets.

"Well, I must say, you wouldn't have a hard time if you

decided to move to a different neighborhood," Ulla observed. She talked with a hint of mockery in her voice, as usual, but the results were not as expected. Her teeth chattered. She was frightened.

"What do you mean by that?" Knut asked suspiciously as he dragged out a piece of string and tied it around the candle.

"What I mean is that you've already packed!"

Knut didn't answer. With great caution he lowered the candle stump down into the hole.

"Here comes a candle, Mickey!" he cried. "Look, shall we go after help? Or should one of us come down and help you? Or what?"

"You mean you have a candle? Wonderful! No, wait a while. I'll take a look at Cecie first. . . ."

The latter words died away into an ununderstandable jumble.

Down below in the cellar Michael, with the lighted candle in hand, had managed to jump down from the cask. He slipped in the mud but fortunately regained his balance. The candle flickered. He bent down over Cecilia.

She lay on her side. He had to creep under the dark shelf in order to shine the light onto her face. Involuntarily, he held his breath as he saw her white cheeks and the dimple in her chin. He held the candle flame up to her mouth. In just a second—it seemed like a year to Michael—the candle began to flicker.

He stood up. He began to move his lips. Gradually his power of speech returned.

"She's breathing!" he shrieked upwards. "She's alive!"

"Alive . . ." Carl Axel managed to stammer. "A-a-alive? Did you think she was dead . . . ?"

Michael looked around. He couldn't make up his mind what to do. Naturally, they could go after help. But he wanted to see Cecilia move . . . talk . . . smile . . . right away!

"Hey up there," he called out. "Try to find a piece of ice for me. Or else pack a snowball—a real hard one—and throw it down. I'll try and see if I can get her conscious."

Ulla's voice answered him from the hole.

"The fellows are making the snowball. Can't I come down there and help you?"

"It's very difficult to get a foothold down here, and it's easy to fall down and get hurt. Also, it's pretty crowded with stuff down here. I think you'd better not."

Very carefully, Michael lifted Cecilia's arm. When he let go, the arm fell down by her side. He found a niche between a couple of planks where he could place the candle. Then he unzipped Cecilia's jacket and loosened her scarf. He felt her wrist and found, to his great relief, that her heartbeat was even and calm.

A couple of inordinately hard snowballs came flying down through the hole. They rolled off under the shelves, but Michael managed to get to one of them. He knelt down beside Cecilia and pressed the snowball first to her temples and then rubbed it lightly over her skin.

As soon as the coldness began to work, Cecilia tried to draw a deep breath. She sighed. Her mouth began to move.

"Cecilia. Wake up. Wake up, Cecie. Can you hear me?"

Terror and anxiety, which had died down when he found that she was still alive, began to mount anew and to a greater degree. How dumb could he be? Working all alone this way. He really should have sent for some help.

He straightened up a bit onto one knee. The melted water from the snowball caused small dirty streams to run down over Cecilia's face. Michael pushed the damp locks of hair from her forehead.

Then her nostrils began to move; her eyelids fluttered. Finally Cecilia opened her eyes. The expression in them was completely vacant at first, and this frightened Michael. But gradually her eyes began to focus and recognition dawned. She blinked and lifted her head a little bit.

Her eyes lighted up. She began to laugh.

Michael, too, tried to laugh, but he failed miserably. All he could manage was a hiccup.

"Can you talk?" he asked. "Do you recognize me?"

Cecilia laughed again. It was a small, funny little laugh.

"Of course I recognize you!" she said, her voice unexpectedly loud and clear. "That's why I'm laughing. You have that old lock of hair falling down in your eyes. It's years since I last saw that!"

12

THE DANCE CLUB

"What did you find down in that old cellar anyway?"

It was Karin Sandberg who had asked.

The other voices quieted down. All eyes turned toward Cecilia. She had sunk into the best upholstered chair in the living room of the Sandberg home. She had on a soft dress made of twill. The flickering light from the open fire made it change color frequently. Cecilia focused her attention on her long, narrow feet and the high-heeled neutral-colored shoes she had on. She noticed everyone directing his attention to her, and, in embarrassment, she pressed her feet one against the other.

"Don't have any idea! I never had time to see what anything looked like, except that there was a huge, terrible old rat walking across the cask just as they hoisted me up through the hole!"

"How awful!"

"I would have died of fright. A wonder that you didn't."

"I can imagine how terrible it must have been."

The cries of the girls drowned out the resounding laughter of the boys.

It was the members of the dance club, established four years previously, who were grouped around the log fire, Cecilia, and a table with fruit and punch.

Actually, the dance club, once a proudly cherished institution, had been like Sleeping Beauty for over a year now. Every single member, boys as well as girls, had complained to himself or to herself over the death of the club, but teen-age shyness had come to the fore and no one had discussed his or her feelings with any of the others. Nobody in Class 4C had dared to bring up the subject and to invite the others over.

Fourteen sets of curious parents had asked many questions:

"What ever happened to your dance club?"

"Isn't it your turn to have the dance club here soon?"

"Aren't you having fun together any longer?"

In fourteen homes, the same answers came out—somewhat sneeringly:

"Aw, nobody wants to bother with it any longer."

"Well, I certainly don't have to invite them if I don't want to!"

"We haven't had any quarrels, really, but we don't go around much together either."

Wide-eyed with astonishment, the parents dropped the subject.

But on that particular Saturday afternoon, the quick-witted Karin Sandberg had seen her chance.

The report of the construction of the snowman, Cecilia's adventure in the cellar, and Michael's rescue of Cecilia had gotten all over town. The telephones buzzed. People on bicycles stopped in front of the post office, the bookstore, and the newsstand to talk.

All the old, forgotten affection for the dance club flared up. The members nodded meaningfully to each other. Michael and Cecilia, who always managed to get themselves into some kind of peculiar situation, were a part of their group. When Karin somewhat uncertainly suggested the club meeting to Carl Axel and Ulla, that was all they needed. In less than an hour the members had contacted one another and the invitation to dance and have some sandwiches and refreshments had been accepted.

All the old gang came—Ulla, Lena, and Brita, Gunilla, Ann Marie, Cecilia herself, Carl Axel, Knut and Michael, Hans and Bengt the twins, Lars and Bertil. The latter, a newcomer a couple of years back, was now a respected pillar of their gang. He was dependability personified. Nobody had to be talked into coming. Nobody was busy. Cecilia had to lie down and rest for a couple of hours, but of course she would be there!

"That old cellar has been there for a good many years. I'm sure there's a lot of junk down there," Knut said.

"What I don't comprehend—what I never have been able to understand really," said the peaceful Brita, "is how it happens that you're always getting into these situations, Cecie. Not once has there ever been a hole in the earth under me that swallows me up, and I faint away . . ."

"And lie down there with all the rats and a bunch of other stuff," Bengt filled in helpfully.

"Oof! And then you were rescued . . . by Michael! . . . and it didn't really do you any damage at all!"

"Well, it has never happened to me before like that either," Cecilia said with a laugh. When she arrived, she had looked a little pale, and there were dark circles under her eyes, but the light from the open fire and the many pairs of interested eyes had somehow caused the color to return to her cheeks. To divert attention from herself, she said, "And what happened to the snowman afterwards? It was really a shame that this had to happen. It was such fun making the snowballs."

"Don't you worry for a minute," Knut said drawlingly. He stretched his legs out in front of him and regarded the toes of his heavy shoes. "I finished him off!"

"Oh, yes. Brag! Brag! And pull in your big, long extremities, Daddy Longlegs!" said Ulla, who was sitting on the floor, tailor-fashion. She lifted one eyebrow. "*We* finished him off before we came over here. And he's a beauty, let me tell you. A bowler hat, a pipe in his mouth, and everything."

"Even if he melts down to nothing tomorrow morning,"

123

said Bertil in a contemplative tone of voice, which, though mild and low, always awakened interest, "he has certainly served his purpose!"

"What do you mean?"

"Well, if it hadn't been for him, none of this business with Cecilia would have happened and we wouldn't have begun talking together just like old times and we wouldn't have been sitting here this evening," Bertil explained.

Carl Axel gave Karin an approving glance.

"It was awfully nice of you to get us all together like this," he said. "Good old dance club! Long live the good old dance club! But tell me"—he suddenly interrupted his train of thought—"why in the world did it go to pot anyway?"

> *"It is not dead; it is sleeping . . .*
> *Its sleep was a century long . . ."*

Hans recited sentimentally. "Now *can* you understand why they told me I was on the borderline between passing and failing in Swedish?"

"Oh, hush," Knut said angrily as he drew in his long legs and sat up straight. "Let's get to the bottom of it. Why *did* it go to pot?"

"Well, *I* can tell you why!" Ulla exclaimed energetically. "That and a whole lot of other things are the fault of Mary Beth. She's an ape!"

As is often the case when a cloud of smoke has long hidden the bitter truth and when all of a sudden the cloud is scattered by a few precise, well-chosen words, the moment of truth caused a deadly silence to fall.

Gunilla slowly but emphatically nodded in agreement, and in the next minute the voice of every girl in the room rose at one time.

"Absolutely right!"

"Ulla's hit on it. She's right!"

"She—Mary Beth—well, I don't know exactly how to explain what I mean, but . . ."

Hans gave voice to the masculine point of view.

"All the gals are jealous of her, but that doesn't change the fact that she's a pretty devastating number—just as Ulla says."

"Hah!" bellowed Carl Axel in his own peculiar fashion— the bellow that had long since ceased to make any impression on his pals. "The girls are all suffering from inferiority complexes."

"And all you guys have spent most of the time fawning over her. Good heavens, the way you fawned!" Ulla's cheeks were beet-red, and in her eagerness to find the precise, biting words she wanted, she almost stammered. "Well, all I've got to say is that I'm eternally grateful that you didn't invite *her* this evening!"

"That would have been all we'd need!" Karin snorted. Her hairdo for the evening was a sort of double pony-tail arrangement. The words seemed to echo out of both sides of her head. "No, she'd never fit in with this bunch!"

"All evening long I've had something in mind," Carl Axel broke in. "Somehow I never got around to it. But now I remember what I meant to do. I've been meaning to lead three cheers for the good old dance club. The dance club! Long live . . . !"

125

Almost spontaneously the fourteen members arose and cheered so loudly that the chandelier in the living room of the Sandberg home shook.

"I think we ought to put something in our glasses," said the hostess as she began to pour. "We can have a toast Lead the cheer once more, Carl Axel!"

"And then," Ulla broke in, "then I think the guys might just keep in mind that this is a *dance* club!"

13

MICHAEL AND CECILIA

In the dining room of the Sandberg home, where the phonograph was located, there was a dormer window, semicircular in shape. It was almost a separate room with its own furniture; there was a nice circle of comfortable chairs. It was to this little room that Cecilia and Michael managed to sneak off in the middle of the first dance.

"There's something I've got to talk over with you right now," Michael had said, "and what I've got to say is very important. I don't think we can dance and talk too."

"No, I noticed that," Cecilia said. "You weren't keeping in step at all."

She was sitting in a huge red wing-chair; her hands were clasped over one knee. Michael leaned over the back of the chair.

"Just a few minutes ago in there," he began softly but with suppressed excitement, "you said that you hadn't seen anything down there in the cellar. Did you really mean that you hadn't seen anything?"

Cecilia looked up; she was puzzled.

"What do you mean? No, of course I didn't see anything. Except for the rat, as I said. And that was more than enough for me."

Michael supported his chin on one of the wings of the chair.

"Well, I can see how that happened. But I had time to take a pretty good look. The candle gave out enough light for me to see a bunch of shelves and a long table. And there were a whole lot of different things on the shelves and on the table."

Michael lowered his voice to a whisper, and Cecilia stared at him wide-eyed.

"What kind of things?"

"Well, that's what I'm coming to. There were long rows of bottles—wine bottles, bottles of soft drinks, and a little of everything. And piles of cigarettes. Just like in a store. It looked just like a newsstand. Just exactly."

Cecilia bolted straight up out of her comfortable position.

"Newsstand?" she said, gasping for breath.

"Yes. It seemed so odd, down there in that old, deserted cellar. And these were new things—expensive things. All of them. And the bottles had never been opened. The seals were still on them."

"Michael! Newsstands!" Cecilia's eyes clouded. "I know just what you're thinking about. The newsstand robberies!"

Michael stood up and moved away from the wing of the chair. He came around in front of Cecilia and sat down on a round, upholstered hassock.

"Yes," he said. "It's obvious that's what I'm thinking about."

It was fairly dark in the little alcove since the only illumination came from a tiny lamp in the form of an old-fashioned lady in red crinoline. Cecilia couldn't actually see the expression on Michael's face, but for a long time now she had been able to recognize every shift in his voice, even when his adolescent voice cracked at times. Without even needing to ask, she realized that he hadn't yet said all he had on his mind.

"Why didn't you say something about it immediately?" she asked in a hushed voice. "If it's as you say it is, you should have told the police."

Michael looked down at his hands.

"Who do you suppose owns that cellar?" he asked.

"Owns? Well, I doubt that anyone in particular *owns* it. I suppose it's on land belonging either to the city or to the lumberyard. There aren't any houses anywhere close to it, if I remember correctly."

"You're right. The land belongs to the city. There's been some talk of their building an atomic bomb shelter there sometime in the future, but you know how long it takes the city to get anything like that under way. The nearest building is the lumberyard."

He stopped talking and leaned forward toward Cecilia.

"That cellar, I'm positive, is left over from ancient times, and I'm equally positive that someone is using it now to hide stolen goods. But who? No doubt somebody who lives in the neighborhood and who stumbled upon it. You remember, don't you, that I told you some time ago that Inspector Nilsson mentioned all these newsstand robberies to me and that he wanted me to help him by keeping my eyes and ears open? He hinted that it might be one of the fellows working at the lumberyard. There were a couple of new employees there he was interested in."

"Michael!"

"Yes, he was. But I never told you how awfully uncomfortable I thought the whole situation was . . . ! You see, I knew that one of the fellows had been in jail once before for robbery and that he is now out on probation. I'm sure the inspector knew all about it, too, but he didn't say anything."

Cecilia turned to look at the little lamp. The tiny lady's skirt, under which the bulb was located, seemed to give off a warm, lovely glow.

"That's terrible," she said quietly. "What a nasty position for you to be in if you have to have any part in putting him back in jail!"

Michael turned his head away. Thoughtfully, he let his fingers move over the contours of the little lamp.

"And he's such a nice guy," Michael said in a clipped fashion. "Really one of the nicest fellows in the whole place. He's helped me more than I can tell you. The work was pretty heavy to begin with, you know."

As had often happened before, both Cecilia and Michael were silent. The silence, however, was not an uncomfortable, beseeching thing; it was calm and pleasant.

From a distance, they heard the voices of their friends.

"Listen. They're playing 'Alexander's Ragtime Band,'" Michael said absent-mindedly. Suddenly he turned to Cecilia.

"Do you think I have to tell the police about the cellar?"

Cecilia put two fingers to her chin.

"I'm sure you've got to," she said with certainty. "Now that you've seen what's down there."

"Yes, you're right. I've simply got to do it."

"But I don't think you need to mention the lumberyard. Perhaps the fellow at the lumberyard will never occur to the police, and you certainly don't have to bring it to their attention."

Michael shook his head.

"They'll think of it themselves, you can bet!" he said sadly. "I don't know. Sometimes you're just unlucky. People will begin to think I'm a professional detective or something of the sort. But it was you who had to go and fall down through the old roof when it comes right down to it!"

He laughed and looked Cecilia in the eye as best he could through the lock of hair that had fallen down over his forehead. Then he suddenly shot up from the hassock.

"Well, in any event, I'll not do anything about talking to Inspector Nilsson before tomorrow morning. . . . Hey, I like ragtime. Do you feel like dancing?"

"Oh, why not!" Cecilia stretched out one hand, and Michael helped her up. "If you can keep step."

14

AS BEFORE

Cecilia went home earlier than the others.

"I had to promise to be home before eleven. Otherwise, they wouldn't have let me come at all," she said with a hint of disappointment in her voice.

"I have a feeling that I ought to go home too," Brita said hesitantly. "We're going to have that awful oral exam in physics on Monday morning."

"Who do you think is going to be concerned with such things this evening, you bookworm, you," said Carl Axel. "Nobody is going to pass it anyway, so you might as well stick with the crowd. If you pass it, you won't have any company at all. You'll be all alone. Come along. I smell hot dogs somewhere."

He grabbed her by the arm, and off they went at full speed.

"Well, good-by, Karin. And thanks a lot for such a good

time." Michael put on his jacket. "I'll walk home with Cecilia and see to it that she doesn't fall down along the way!"

"You don't really need to . . ." Cecilia protested weakly.

"I certainly do need to. I wouldn't dream of letting you walk home alone."

As they walked down the hill, the good-by choruses of the others followed them. In addition, those who stood along the balcony threw a good many snowballs in their direction.

"I think Hans is trying to get them to sing a serenade," Cecilia said with a giggle. "Good heavens, it's pretty cold out here, isn't it?"

Michael took her by the arm. He continued to hold her arm even after they had reached the road. This made Cecilia feel much more sure-footed; she wasn't used to walking in the snow with high heels.

"And at this time of night, nobody is out on the streets," she thought.

They walked along below the Nordvik castle. Its silhouette seemed massive and heavy against the background of blinking stars.

"You weren't there the last time we had lab period in physics, were you?" said Michael as he gave out a bellow of laughter. "I thought at the time that I'd have to remember to tell you because you usually enjoy such things so much. Well, anyway, we were talking about how much a meter is—you know, the business about a meter being

134

'the distance between two certain points on the imperial measuring standard in Paris.' "

"Yes, yes. I know," Cecilia said. "I can say it in my sleep."

"Can't we all! The teacher asks the question at every possible opportunity so we'll all get it into our heads. But the last time, you see, we had studied horsepower, and Knut got asked what we mean by horsepower. And you know how Knut is. He was sitting there thinking of something totally different, of course. He stared sort of sleepily straight ahead, and then he began to speak. 'Horsepower is the power that is discharged by . . . by . . . an imperial horse . . .' Then he stopped, of course, because he could tell that what he had said sounded a little peculiar, but then he got an inspiration and said, 'An imperial horse in Paris!' And brother, did we ever laugh! Even the teacher had to laugh. Actually, I thought he was going to fall off his chair!"

Cecilia also laughed.

They were still laughing when they reached a bend in the road and found themselves face to face with their old friend, Colonel Malm. They were just passing under a street lamp, and of course he recognized them immediately. Cecilia thought to herself that Michael would surely let go of her arm, but he didn't. He just removed his cap, and Cecilia curtsied.

"Hello, you two," the Colonel said. However, he didn't stop to talk. His dachshund was pulling too eagerly on the leash.

All of a sudden, Cecilia and Michael began to relive old memories—memories of their first days in the Coeducational School when they hardly knew each other. Things they had thought about, felt about. Things they liked. All sorts of things. And about the Colonel.

Cecilia had never thought it possible that you could talk to a boy this way. Certainly, you could with your girl friends. Still and all, it wasn't quite the same, she guessed, because she noticed that she and Michael often had quite differing views on this and that, while, with the girls, they almost always shared the same point of view.

With a boy it was even more fun. It was like paddling out from shore, coming back, and seeing the same old bays, hills, and meadows from a totally different direction.

It was quite clear to them, as they approached the gate to Cecilia's house, that they weren't quite talked out yet, and Cecilia invited Michael to come in.

Out in the kitchen they squeezed some lemons and oranges—they were thirsty—and then they sat down and talked until midnight.

Strangely enough, no one in the house woke up. What a contrast, Cecilia thought, to that night when Knut and Ramrod had paid them a visit. She described the evening to Michael. Michael, in turn, told about his adventure with Mary Beth and her brother and about the motorcycle gang and the business with the police near Lindeby.

After Michael had gone, Cecilia walked about the kitchen, straightening up the mess. She was smiling to herself. All of a sudden, she felt sleepy—warmly, wonderfully sleepy.

Up in her room she opened her window and undressed in the dark. She had had in mind to read the latest issue of one of her magazines before going to sleep, but she realized she had no desire to read.

Instead, she crawled in between the sheets, turned over on her side, and looked out the window at the old, familiar black trees and the small triangle of the sky. Into her path of vision came briskly moving clouds at the precise moment she crossed the threshold between being barely conscious and fast asleep.

And Michael?

Well, Michael wasn't really sleepy, and all around him the world seemed alert and alive. The cold, the snow that squeaked under the soles of his shoes, the icy, lacy quality of the treetops, the impenetrable darkness of the yards— all these seemed to Michael to be just as alive, just as violently active and glittering as the stars themselves. He felt a surge of power. He felt that he could keep going all night long.

It even seemed quite appropriate that this wondrous silence was suddenly broken by some gusts of wind from the bay. At first, the wind seemed to be merely a soft breeze coming from the pine forest, but gradually the wind broke through all the barriers and began to sweep across the land from the sea. As Michael approached the Shore Promenade, he realized it had gotten much colder, and he noticed that the stars were concealed by groups of fast-moving, heavy clouds. But this was all right. The wind brought with it that necessary small hint of adventure and danger—something that had been missing when it was so calm.

He walked along the Shore Promenade toward the residential area of the bay, and he made a mental note to put his name down for the "Try to Fly Day," to which the boys in the intermediate grades had been invited. In the space of a moment, however, his fantasies were interrupted.

There was something wrong here along the bay.

Most of the houses lay in utter darkness. After all, it was past twelve-thirty. The cross street below the houses was, as usual, not too well lighted; there was just one street light in the middle of the traffic safety zone.

All this appeared to be in order.

But some distance back from the cross street was located one of the stores in the Nordvik dairy chain—a new building that looked like a barracks. On one side lay what had once been a railroad yard, now overgrown with weeds and cluttered up with junk; on the other side was another vacant lot. The building that had formerly stood there had burned to the ground a few years ago. The fact that the ground was swampy and that the landscape was anything but attractive had scared away most construction companies or real estate speculators.

Michael knew good and well that this entire triangle occupied by the dairy store and the two vacant lots was usually in utter darkness.

But now it wasn't dark. Something was going on in the

139

dairy. There were lights in the store, the doors were open, and dark figures were moving around inside—some in the wing and some in the main part of the store.

Struck with amazement, Michael slackened his pace. He took a couple of fast steps to one side in order to get behind a couple of low spruce trees. Thoughts raced through his head.

Was it perhaps a late delivery of provisions to the dairy store?

On a Saturday night? Impossible!

Was there a fire? Were the firemen having fire-prevention practice?

Was it a robbery?

Every nerve in Michael's body was on edge.

He noticed that a car, with no lights, was parked right by the wing of the store—the one that faced the old railroad yard. He thought he could also make out the contours of a motorcycle. It occurred to him that it might be a policeman's motorcycle, but the fact that the car's lights weren't on and that the vehicle was parked in there among the thistles and bushes caused him to cast that idea aside.

Up to now he had been more curious than afraid. He kept telling himself that it was a habit of his to be suspicious of anything the least out of the ordinary.

He hurried along quickly and purposefully, with no pretense of being cautious, to a little shed once used by an attendant at the railway yard, but nowadays used mainly for advertising posters. It was located just opposite

140

the dairy store, something like fifty yards from the door.

And now he could hear voices, but in spite of the fact that he strained every nerve to the utmost, all he could hear was a jumble of incoherent sounds.

Other sounds reached his ears—the creaking of a door; bottles clanking together; and once a noise that seemed strangely out of place in this whole seemingly-carefully-planned production, a girl's laugh.

The other side of the railroad-yard shed was in total darkness because of its position close to a wooden wall bordered by thorny bushes. From that side he could get a much better view of what was going on.

Michael rounded the corner. By now his movements were quick, noiseless, and watchful as they always were when he sensed that real danger was at hand.

No longer did he stop to argue with himself. He was absolutely certain that he was witnessing a robbery.

Crouching down in the snow among the bushes—actually, he was down on all fours, not remembering that he had on his very best slacks—he automatically took note of several important points for future use. The car parked at the wing was a very dark, probably black, Volkswagen. He couldn't make out the license number. In back of the car, at the corner nearest Michael, was a motor scooter. As far as the dark figures were concerned, they were moving around so much and so fast that at first it seemed impossible to count how many there were. Finally, Michael counted at least four, and from all he could judge, they were young people.

Michael was astonished at their audacity. The store, where the thieves had put on the lights and were moving around so unconcernedly, was fully visible from at least three houses on the other side of the thoroughfare. To be sure, these houses were dark, all was quiet around them, and two of the houses were partly hidden by enormously tall fir trees. But in any case, it seemed very risky in the face of the fact that someone in any of the houses might awaken.

Furthermore, somebody might have come by along the road. Naturally, this wasn't a much-trafficked street, but even at that, the robbers were taking a big chance.

The approximate strength of their forces suddenly became clear to Michael. Everything seemed to be happening at top speed. Both doors of the car were opened, and the loading operation was steady and quick. Michael heard the clinking of the bottles as carrying cases with bottles in them were placed in the back compartment, and he saw the figures rushing between the store and the car.

In just a couple of minutes the whole picture was quite clear to him. A chain of thoughts began forming in his brain. The strength of the gang was much larger than he had at first imagined. In the light from large battery searchlights, they worked at a great rate; soon they'd be ready and would probably disappear into the darkness of the old railway yard, then find their way onto one of the many winding, crossing paths or roads beyond the railroad.

Michael had no difficulty in determining precisely what was taking place, but what could he do about it? Go back along the Shore Promenade? Even if he managed to break all racing records in the snow, it would take him at least five minutes to get to the nearest house in that direction, five minutes more to wake its occupants and explain the situation, and some additional precious minutes to telephone the police, and more minutes before the police could get going. . . .

Michael hit his clenched fists against his knees. By that time the thieves would be far away from Nordvik. They might already have reached their hiding place—or they would soon—wherever that place might be. . . .

No, the only way to get any help would be to go to one of the houses on the other side of the road. And in order to get there . . .

Then it happened.

Someone turned on a light in the upper story of the nearest of the houses—the one that had the best view of the road below. A window was raised.

Someone besides Michael had realized what was happening. Two of the thieves, who were carrying a load between them, found themselves on the steps outside the store just at that moment. They stopped dead in their tracks. The others inside stopped whatever they were doing. It occurred to Michael that perhaps they were busy taking a look at the cash register. But would anyone leave a lot of money around in a store over the weekend? He knew so little when he needed to know so much. It was scarcely believable that there would be much money. Maybe some small change.

143

Someone called out from the open window across the way. It was a woman's voice.

A window is sometimes a very eloquent thing. It looked just as if a house had opened one sleepy eye, been surprised, become wide awake in the space of a second, and was now beginning to emit streams of activity.

Lights went on downstairs as well. Michael could imagine the traffic on the stairs, excited voices, buzzing telephone wires.

A new shout pierced the air. It was carried along by a gust of wind, but the only thing Michael could make out there in the bushes was the last faint word.

". . . there?"

The awareness that help might be on the way, that someone else was doing something about all this, electrified Michael. He got up and ran forward a few yards in the direction of the center of events.

From there he could see that everything was being done in a colossal hurry. As they put the last case into the car, one of the figures rushed back into the store.

With no real plan of what he might be able to do but with a definite feeling that he had to do something, Michael crept along through the snow, covering the few yards that lay between him and the wing of the building. He held himself close to the wall with its regular pattern of grayish stones, which were cemented together with some sort of shiny material.

The car stood just a little farther away toward the other corner, and there beside him, so close that he could have touched it, was the motorcycle.

Suddenly the lights were all turned off. But in that frighteningly impenetrable darkness, sounds became unexpectedly eloquent.

Voices raised in excitement; many swear words. Once more a girl's laugh, shrill, piercing. The sound of a pane of glass being broken. Running steps crossing over the broken glass. The buzz of a car motor, waiting dutifully, expectantly.

All the while Michael got the impression that the robbers were calm and collected and that their work, in spite of some confusion caused by the darkness, was accomplished with astounding precision and cold-bloodedness. The recurring sound of a commanding voice seemed to spread an atmosphere of discipline and caution that precluded any possibility of sudden panic.

To a certain degree Michael could understand why. The police station was more than a mile away. The thieves didn't have much time to spare, but they had time enough to get away. The lone feminine voice from the house on the other side of the road had not caused any sudden outbreak of fear.

But neither was Michael in the mood to be panicky. He was surprised to find that his feeling of hopelessness and helplessness had disappeared; he had had time to recharge his batteries.

It was obvious that the police would arrive too late. And of course it would take them a while to examine any clues that the thieves might have left behind them.

There was only one thing that Michael felt he could try, and that was to follow the thieves as they got away.

If they were the same people who were being sought in connection with the other robberies, they would be, at least according to the police, from the neighboring territory. Maybe the chase wouldn't take very long.

At the same moment the pane of glass was broken, Michael placed his hands on the handle bars of the motor scooter. During the few seconds when all seemed utter confusion in the face of the darkness and the broken glass, Michael flexed his muscles and managed to kick up the stand, which was constructed along the same lines as the one on Peter Evander's old motor scooter. Pulling the machine with him over the open ground, he rushed back to his previous hiding place. This whole long white stretch, where, in spite of the darkness, his silhouette could be seen by any observer, seemed unending. His imagination caused a little feeling of terror to go through him: Was it possible that the robbers were armed?

He crouched down, half prepared to hear bullets whistle any minute. Finally he reached the shelter of the shed. Michael almost disappeared in a huge bank of snow and nearly fell down with the scooter on top of him, but he managed to keep his balance and covered the few remaining yards, reaching the other side of the shed in a couple of leaps. He turned the motor scooter around and placed it against the wall. In no time he lay flat on the ground, peering back at the dairy store. Well, this was it! Had he been discovered? Had they followed him? If that were the case, the only thing to do was to leave the motor scooter to its own destiny and run for his life.

No. There seemed to be no immediate danger, at least.

The snow-covered area between the buildings was deserted.

Michael began to breathe very hard. He felt as if he had forgotten to breathe for a long while.

Michael caught his breath.

Good heavens! Look at the tracks that had been left behind—by him and the scooter! If the thieves decided to follow, that would be the last of him!

It was impossible to see what was going on over there. At this point they certainly had very little time to lose. Michael knew from experience that the police were very quick to appear where they were needed. And for that matter, a radio car might have been out on patrol and be somewhere in the neighborhood.

Something was happening! Ah, yes. There was the buzz of the car motor, and the lights of the car went on. Michael stiffened, prepared to run. There was also a powerful searchlight, the beams from which seemed to dance mockingly across the drifts of snow, the dark tracks of tires and footprints, and the railroad-yard's shed. How in the world could he have imagined that such a simple ruse as trying to get away with the motor scooter would be successful?

There they came—one—two!

Nothing to do but try to escape!

At that moment a cry and a signal came from the car.

His pursuers halted.

Time—this was his greatest ally!

They turned. Hundreds of swear words seemed to fly like rockets over the snow.

At this point Michael indulged in a happy grin from ear to ear.

"Well, now. Serves you right!" he muttered between his teeth. "How are you going to find room for everybody now?"

15

THE PURSUIT

Loud voices confirmed the fact that the matter of crowding everyone into the small car and getting away had now become acute. Then the car doors were closed once more.

Michael's ears interpreted these sounds, but all the while he moved his cold, but astonishingly sure fingers over the control panel of the scooter. There was just one chance in a hundred that he would be able to get it started and take up the chase.

If it were only like Peter's old motor scooter. Every detail of that seemed to have been engraved on a map that lay deep in Michael's head. But of course Peter's scooter had some sort of special construction.

In his mind's ear, he could hear Mary Beth's droll voice —dry, but still very feminine: "The brakes are located here. Now, let's turn on the lights. Bright . . . and dim!"

Strangely enough, he wasn't surprised to find the key

precisely where it should be. He turned it with one hand. With the other he felt around for the switch.

Mentally he went over the details of the steering mechanism, and he knew that he wasn't imagining things. The grip was familiar. The shallow grooves of the rubber handgrippers, the location of the signals. It was the same model of motor scooter—or, to be more accurate, a cross between a motor scooter and a motorcycle—on which he had practiced that memorable evening down on the stony ground at Ekenase.

Michael's hands stopped moving. For a moment he tried to figure out what all this meant—tried to . . .

Beams of light spread out across the road leading from the railroad yard. Michael hopped into the saddle. He put one foot on the starter pedal. With his fingers he controlled the gas.

Through his body went the wonderful feeling that he was in control of the situation. He leaned forward across the steering mechanism.

The car was coming. The headlights seemed to split the darkness like a pair of angry cat eyes. Just as Michael had expected, they took the road that crossed the tracks, went under a viaduct, and took off in the direction of the wooded area that lay back of them.

Michael pumped the starter with his foot—once—twice. More gas. Of course. It's much colder now. The third time. Ah!

"Good boy," he said to himself.

The motor scooter—Michael began to regard it as an

old friend—lurched wildly as he crossed a sunken place in the snow, but he managed to hold it upright.

Thirty-five miles an hour, Mary Beth had said. On these narrow, curving roads through the woods, they wouldn't be able to do much better with their Volkswagen! But whoever was driving had a lot of nerve. That was clear when they took the first curve under the viaduct, but they skidded.

Michael smiled as he accelerated. The condition of the roads was against them, too!

He wasn't much more than fifty yards behind the speeding car as he emerged from under the viaduct. He decided to put a little more distance between himself and the car.

A few days before the bitter cold had swept in over the bay, it had rained almost without stopping. The roads had been thoroughly soaked, muddy, and full of ruts, and that was the condition in which they had frozen. Michael discovered that he was forced to use all his powers of concentration, plus every ounce of strength in his arms, to keep the motor scooter upright, even at a moderate speed.

The road the thieves had taken was used mostly as a walking path or a riding path. It seemed to curve around the slightest elevation. The red rear lights on the Volkswagen disappeared time after time as they went around curves, only to reappear, like teasing eyes, between the trees. There was no question that they would not be able to travel at very high speed with as many curves as there were along the road. But Michael was aware that the thieves, in spite of their handicaps, had chosen wisely.

They took no chance of meeting either the police or anybody else.

It was obvious that they knew their way around the territory. Conscious of just what they were doing, they plowed ahead without hesitating at crossroads, and they made use of every straight stretch to go along at a much higher speed.

A treacherous rut, caused by a wheel, almost made Michael fall. He was thrown violently to one side and took the shock with his left foot. A shooting pain flew from his heel to his knee and began to go all the way up to his thigh. Finally, when he was able to get going again and had reached the top of the next hill, he discovered that his guiding lights—the red lights on the rear of the car—had disappeared.

Michael gave the scooter too much gas. His heart was beating wildly. He began to feel that it was an almost

independent mechanism—one that wanted to get out of its cage in among his ribs.

The motor scooter made it over the top of the hill. Here the woods ended and wilderness territory began. The snow had filled the ditches along the side, but it had blown away from the rough edges of the ruts.

The road led downward, with another curve in it. Michael took it with such style that his confidence grew. Even if the thieves knew the terrain well, he knew it no less well. After all the cross-country runs he had done with the school team, he could almost have made a map of the woods around Nordvik.

Once on the other side of this huge rock, he would be able to see quite a distance down the road. Now if only the Volkswagen hadn't disappeared again.

It hadn't. There it was. Those guiding red lights.

Michael made a face in the darkness. He forgot all

about the stiffness and pain in his leg. Everything was as he had calculated. At this point the thieves turned into what was little more than a footpath. Michael knew it inside out. It led through a glen, past a couple of gardens, to a wooded area covered by hazel trees, at the end of which was the foot of the hill leading to the castle. He let up on the gas. He certainly didn't need to risk discovery by following the speeding car too closely. No longer was there any doubt in his mind—it was heading toward the vacant lot beyond the school—to the cellar with its suspicious contents.

Deliberately he let his prey disappear between the hazel bushes.

He needed time to think.

Should he return to the dairy store and bring back the police, who must surely have reached the scene by this time? He wouldn't be able, all alone, to accomplish much over there by the cellar.

On the other hand, it was possible that the thieves, who knew that the robbery had been discovered and that they might be followed, might hastily unload the car and then disappear without leaving any tracks at all. They would almost have time to get away before he could return with the police.

No, the best thing would be to follow them clear to the cellar, get the license number of the car, which he had not as yet been able to make out, and get a good description of all of them. There would be many good hiding places there among the bushes and thickets in the overgrown vacant lot.

Mixed feelings of happiness and excitement flew through Michael's body. He thought of his friend—the melancholy, reserved fellow at the lumberyard—whom he might now be able to help by discovering the real thieves. It was a whole gang who had worked together back there at the dairy store. In his mind's ear Michael could still hear the echo of the girl's laughter as it rose shrilly above the jumble of voices and words of command during the robbery.

And the motor scooter, which he had been lucky enough to confiscate, belonged to Mary Beth.

Disjointed sentences flew around in his head, just as clearly as if they had been spoken right here in the white forest:

"Let's get out of here!"

"You idiot!"

"We're just out riding for the fun of it!"

"So, I guess you know everybody in town, huh?"

Michael clicked his teeth together. He simply had to get that license number. And as far as the description was concerned . . .

Suddenly he could see the silhouette of the castle as the road through the woods came to an end. After a slight bend that led around a small hill, covered with a cushion of anemones in the spring, it led up to the broad paved highway, which separated the school hill from the castle hill.

Michael turned off the motor and led the motor scooter slowly in between the piles of snow left by the plows.

There was no trace of the car; not a person was to be

seen. The old-fashioned street lights cast their glow down upon the roadway. In their light you could see part way along a smaller road that led past the overgrown lot up to the red buildings of the lumberyard. Carefully he rolled the motor scooter along the footpath. Turning his ear toward the center of the lot, where the cellar lay, he listened intently.

The sea breezes were no longer mild and unprepossessing; now they were powerful and impatient, just like the breath coming from the chest of an irritated giant.

A spruce hedge bordered the road. For many years school children who were late had made holes through this prickly natural barrier. Soon Michael found a hole at the end of a trampled-down path in the snow, and it was big enough for him and the motor scooter both to pass through. Inside the hedge he stood for a moment, peering, listening. The branches of the trees and the thickets waved and rustled in the wind, which seemed bent upon filling every cranny with its own ill will. The snow, which had come to rest on bushes and trees, was stirred up by the gusts; as the last part of its appointed task, the wind whizzed up the hill toward the wing of the school building.

The wind carried sounds with it. Michael could finally make out the weak hum of a car motor. The motor was idling.

He let the motor scooter fall down in the direction of the hedge—the dry branches crackled as it fell. That done, he went forward, bending over a little, but with rapid and sure steps, in among the fruit trees. A couple of times he sank down deep in invisible holes and hollows, but he managed not to deviate from his intended path. Here were the grassy mounds where they used to play cops and robbers in the first and second years of school. And that must be the silhouette of the old pear tree. Farther up was the school. He imagined more than saw its old familiar shape.

Through the bushes he suddenly caught sight of one of the tail lights. He stepped hastily to one side because he had not been prepared to see it so suddenly nor to have it be so close. He smiled as he clenched his fists inside his coat pockets.

Apparently the thieves were pretty sure of themselves since they hadn't turned off the lights!

Now he could make out the rounded top on the Volkswagen.

It was the parking lights that were on, but they furnished enough illumination to light up the narrow passage to the cellar door.

Michael crouched down. Silently he went a few steps farther. In an angle between the trees, he could see the lighted license plate. Eagerly he looked. He could see the numbers: 98089. That was an easy number to remember! The letter in front of the numbers was covered by slush, but a curved line at the bottom seemed to be part of a "B."

It was a black car. Just as before, back at the dairy store, both doors of the car were open. Michael began to think it resembled a bird, its wings ready for instantaneous flight once the sign had been given.

He could hear voices from inside the cellar. No longer

157

did they seem so excited; the jumble of sounds seemed to be filled with self-confidence and rose, now and then in a resounding, triumphant laugh.

At this point Michael began to tire of hearing only the sounds of voices. To be sure, he had gotten the license number, and within him rose the feeling that he had been the winner of the last round. This feeling, in turn, caused other feelings to come to the surface: fearlessness, a sense of combat, curiosity. He wanted to—he just had to—see at least one of the thieves, not as a dark, vague shadow but clearly, so clearly that later on he could say with certainty, "I recognize him! He's the one I saw!" Or her . . .

In addition, it was possible that this was a stolen car that they might later on abandon in some ditch while the members of the gang dispersed and went their separate ways.

In just a matter of seconds, Michael had decided upon a plan.

Almost creeping, he speedily made his way along under the branches. He came so close to the Volkswagen that he could reach out with his hand and touch the bumper. Continuing along, he found himself once more among the thickets, then around the foot of the hill where the cellar was located. He caught sight of the dark hole into which Cecilia had fallen earlier that day, or yesterday, to be exact. Was it really only yesterday! What had the thieves thought when they discovered that there had been visitors in their cellar? Perhaps the self-assurance in their voices took a downward turn for a few seconds.

And there he was—the snowman. Magnificent. Safe and sound.

Michael laughed to himself. The snowman would make a perfect hiding place. Now he could really serve a purpose!

As he had promised, Knut had been responsible for the artistic, decorative touches on the snowman. He had furnished him with a bowler hat, a little pipe, and a shrewd, teasing, mysterious expression on his face. Amazing what artistic fingers can accomplish with a few pieces of coal!

For a brief moment, Michael forgot about the drama that was taking place down in the cellar and approached the snowman.

Against the fast-moving clouds and the starry sky he looked very odd—a frozen black-and-white statue, with a lifeless but almost knowing moon-round face.

Standing there on the hill, Michael had braced himself with one foot against a stone. Suddenly the stone came loose and rolled across the frozen ground. Michael stumbled. It must have been this unexpected turn of events that made him think he heard a sound coming from the snowman. The sound was that of someone drawing a deep breath. Yes, it must have come from the snowman!

Michael attempted to find a foothold and a moment later came one step closer to the motionless white figure.

Could it be the stars that were visible now and then as they peered from behind the moving clouds; could it be the excitement of the last half hour; or was it the cold that caused him to see spots before his tired eyes?

Michael didn't have time to lift an arm to protect himself.

His only thought was that the hard-packed white snowballs, which he himself had helped to roll, had come to life and lunged at him, causing black-and-white sparks to fly.

As he felt a terrible blow on the head, black and white changed to red, to green, to yellow, and back to red again. Blood red. Just like a heavy curtain that fell over his eyes, his ears, and all his senses.

He felt as if he were falling and falling and falling. How could the distance to the ground be so tremendous? . . . He continued to fall. The red spots disappeared. Icy blue ones appeared instead; little by little even these lost their color and became white—the whiteness of endlessness and of terror. The whiteness of nothing.

16

RAMROD AGAIN

That night Nordvik resembled a frozen panorama. Houses and cottages, business buildings and shacks—everything that had been made by the hand of man—stood out in sharp relief against a background where the smiles of nature had turned to stone. Later on there came an absolute stillness that spread out like a net over the roads, the paths, and the public meeting places.

But nowhere was the silence as deep as it was across the overgrown vacant lot. Motionless, the snowman stood there, his hat on the ground nearby. Motionless, too, was the dark figure down below—strangely thin, as if it had been reduced in size by the glistening whiteness of the surroundings.

The mercury fell and fell. Even the wind from the sea seemed hampered by the biting cold.

The snow began to fall, not in soft, fluffy star-shaped flakes—the kind you wish for at Christmas—not in soggy clumps, as sometimes happens in the spring, but in hard, stony spikes and grains, which were unpleasant and which caused your skin to sting. They found their way to Michael's torn jacket and his dark trousers. They made their way to his bare head, his throat, and his unprotected ears. They crept in among all the folds of his clothing, settled down and began to pack themselves together. These were the storm troopers of real winter, tiny but armed with their own special weapons; these were hardness personified, and their job was to freeze—to cause anything in their path to freeze to death.

They welcomed their defenseless prey. They were contented to accomplish their mission without interruption.

Here, in among the thickets, they felt safe and secure. Who in the world would come along to disturb them at a time like this when the whole population of Nordvik was asleep, including even the fox, that stout-hearted fighter, who usually didn't spend much of the nighttime in his lair but roamed, instead, over the whole territory near the shore?

But hush! Wasn't that a noise in the hedge? Could he have decided to roam around in any case, tempted, perhaps, by the young, fat pheasant hens?

No. It wasn't the pointed, cruel nose of the fox that was rooting around in the newly fallen snow.

It was a broad, kindly nose, carefully, thoughtfully making a path through the thickets.

There was a snort. An old, familiar snort.

Ramrod!

Ramrod had had a very successful Saturday evening. He had been down visiting with his lady love on the other side of the castle; with a violent shake of his head he had taken off after a dachshund, a spaniel, and a sensitive but brave collie; he had followed them at wild speed.

And that wasn't all. He had been permitted to enter the vestibule at Cleo's house, where he was admired and petted by all the children in the household and where he had been fed the remains of some marvelous hash. Cleo hadn't raised any objections to this; in fact, she had simply stood there looking more beautiful than ever.

Ramrod sensed that he was well on the way to making a conquest.

But as evening turned to deep night, his luck had not been as good.

His head still reeling over his newly found happiness, Ramrod finally went home only to find the friendly yellow house—his home where he received food and shelter—dark and locked up tight.

Ramrod barked and barked. Standing on his hind legs, he banged against the door, but no one in the house showed a single sign of life.

What had happened, of course, was that Knut's parents were away, and Knut himself was dancing any number of "last dances" with Karin Sandberg.

Ramrod was disappointed, but he was far from distressed. He was still warm all over because his happiness was so great, and he felt much confidence in himself. The gusts of wind from the east were, for him, just mild breezes. He filled his ample lungs with air to such an extent that his ribs almost rattled, whereupon he decided to go down and find out if the cat had returned to the old vacant lot. . . .

And maybe he remembered, too, what fun he and Knut had had playing in the snow at noontime. Who knows? Maybe Knut would be down there now.

Ramrod took off at a trot. He cut across the yards, crept under the fences, and went over a stone wall in one magnificent leap. He finally crawled around a nest of barbed wire in the old lot. And what should reach his nose but the scent of Michael—a highly pleasant and encouraging smell, which filled him with assurance. In Ramrod's mind, the smell of Michael was inextricably tied up with that of Knut. To be sure, it was a strange time of night for games, but who can understand the minds of boys? For Ramrod, the boys took on the form of gods, and you were not supposed to understand their method of operation or to criticize them; you simply accepted them. That was the price you had to pay for the privilege of owning a master. . . .

In a couple of wild, blissful leaps, he reached the snowman. Noticing the hat, he managed, with one carefully calculated jump, to knock it high into the air. It rolled down the slope, and Ramrod gratefully took up the game. Pushing the front part of his body down into the snow, he began to yelp like a small puppy. He pretended that the hat was a dangerous, enchanted monster. His red tongue, hanging from his gaping mouth, looked like fire; the breath coming from his mouth looked like puffballs.

But of course it was absolutely impossible to play all by yourself in such freezing weather.

Ramrod stood with one forepaw lifted high in the air.

Suddenly his nose caught a new and especially strong wave of Michael's scent; simultaneously he saw something dark in the snow. He rushed over.

At first he was so happy that he didn't know what to do. Here was his friend Michael. And he was playing dead for Ramrod's benefit, just as he had done so many times in the past.

"Hey, Michael. Here I am!" the dog seemed to say.

"Look, don't kid me any longer. Hey, get up. We can have lots of fun if you'll just stand up. Hey, get up. I say, get up. Don't you recognize me? It's your old friend. Ramrod."

But the dark figure remained motionless. Ramrod made one last brave attempt to put his nose against Michael's neck, which was pretty well covered with snow.

Suddenly Ramrod seemed to sense that something was wrong. He sat down on his hind legs and made a sudden motion involving both helplessness and disappointment. In a split second his mood had changed.

Loneliness, the silence, and the cold engulfed him in sudden, heavy waves. To top it all, he caught sight of the moon, which had suddenly appeared at an angle above the dark roof of the schoolhouse. The piece of galvanized metal gleamed in its light; it highlighted the bald pate of the snowman. Slowly it spread its light over Ramrod's lifeless friend who lay at his feet.

This was just too much for Ramrod. Even under the best conditions, Ramrod had never cared much for the moon. And now it caused his canine heart to overflow with a feeling of anxiety, a feeling of helplessness. Stretching his neck, he lifted his head toward the sky and let out a long, mournful yowl—a strange wild cry having little to do with the tame, friendly dog from Nordvik. It seemed to be a noise coming from the ice age, carrying overtones of wild tundra, a noise emanating from some long-forgotten, deep part of his soul.

He had made this noise so suddenly and it had been so loud and had sounded so strange to Ramrod that he was almost scared out of his wits.

He jumped up and ran around in a couple of aimless circles, remembered, to his mounting terror, that his home was locked and deserted, and took off down the slope in precisely the opposite direction. His departure was at such a speed that the newly fallen dry snow whirled as his paws stirred it up. He flew through the gooseberry bushes, scratched his forehead on the barbed wire, and, at last, found himself galloping along the frozen road.

There was a definite destination he had in mind. His instinct brought something to the surface: the memory of an autumn evening when he was bleeding and whimpering and Knut led him through these same roads to a white house behind a hedge where some squirrels lived.

Inside that white house there had been warmth and light, soft feminine hands, a kitchen with lovely smells and a wondrous bone, the like of which he had never seen before.

Ramrod was a born optimist. The nearer he came to the white house, the more crystallized these memories became in his mind. He was sure the girl would be at home and equally sure that she would come down and open the door, that she would welcome him with open arms.

Ramrod covered the ground leading to Cecilia's house in record time. When he rushed through the gate, all doubts disappeared, and he was happy and confident. Not even the dark windows and the closed door could possibly dampen his animal spirits.

After all, it had looked just like this the last time, too!

Appraising the situation, he looked up at the sleeping house. Then he rushed around to the place where he and Knut had stood the time before. In other words, he had decided to take up his position beneath Cecilia's window, where he gave vent to his feelings of triumph by letting out a yell that split the silence of the night.

Ramrod's bark was unique—all the more so when he was wildly excited, as he was now. His "woofs" didn't come out in staccatos but, because they came out in such a hurry, blended together in a single long phrase: "Woo-oo-oo-oo-oo-oof!" This demanded so much effort that the front part of his body was raised, and he stood there pawing the air. Long ago he had discovered that a bark such as this seldom failed to accomplish its intended purpose.

And it didn't fail this time, either.

There was a noise in the hedge as the animals, not visible to the naked eye, moved around. An owl lifted its wings and flew from the top of the house. On the other side of the road, a pheasant family came to life and began a disturbed cackling.

And Cecilia flew out of bed. Even before she managed, though she was still half asleep and her fingers were trembling, to open the window wide, she was sure that it must be Ramrod who had been responsible for this noctural explosion of sound.

"What's going on? Hey!"

Cecilia rubbed her eyes.

Sure enough. There he was. In vain, she tried to see Knut's figure among the shadows on the snow-covered ground.

Ramrod let out another yell. This time, glad to be recognized, his bark was even louder. He had known it all the time. Here lived a lovely girl who was usually awake!

"Ramrod! Are you out of your mind? Where are you keeping Knut? Look, go on home! You'll wake up everybody in the house!"

The sound of Knut's name—the name of his beloved master—made Ramrod even more excited. He sat down in a snowdrift underneath Cecilia's window and continued to bark loudly.

He was barking because it was cold, because he was hungry, because Michael was still over there, motionless in the snow, and because Cecilia mentioned Knut's name and told Ramrod to go home.

He was, in addition, baying at the moon.

Cecilia shut the window. She grabbed her snow pants

and put them on over her nightgown. Over her head she pulled her heavy Icelandic sweater.

Ten to one that Knut was hiding somewhere down there. Maybe the others were along too. Somehow, at this time of night, her friends seemed to get the craziest ideas.

But listen to that dog bark. She simply had to quiet him; otherwise, the whole family would soon be up. It was a wonder that the smaller children hadn't awakened already.

After she had put on a pair of wool socks, Cecilia felt her way down the stairs. In the hall she found her leather boots and stuck her feet into them. A moment later, with trembling fingers, she took off the chain and unlocked the door.

Right on the stone steps, Ramrod gave her an overwhelming greeting and show of affection.

He had been right all the time. She did have wonderfully soft hands, that girl.

In vain, Cecilia peered around in the darkness.

"Ramrod! Good heavens! Take it easy. Calm down, I said. Where are you hiding Knut?"

At that point Ramrod sat down and began to lick his nose.

Unable to make up her mind, Cecilia looked all around. What was she going to do with the dog? Maybe she could telephone Knut at home.

But it was so awfully late! What if his parents had gone to bed? And what if his father answered the telephone, angry because he had been wakened out of a sound sleep?

"Excuse me, this is Cecilia Acker. Is Knut there?"

Cecilia blushed wildly at the very thought. She would rather die. Rather do almost anything.

And besides, it was a breath-takingly beautiful night—cold and clear. Now that she was wide awake, Cecilia remembered that she had a good many wonderful things to think about. Her rescue from the cellar; the dance at the Sandberg house; the way Michael looked at her now and then. . . . These are the things you want to think about when you go out for a walk, all alone except for a dog, in the middle of the night.

17

"GO AFTER THE SNOWMAN!"

No beef bone was forthcoming, but Ramrod was still quite contented.

No longer was he alone; and he had forgotten all about the moon. In every possible way he tried to tell Cecilia that he thought she was utterly charming and that never again did he want to be separated from her. He managed to show her his feelings partly by finding delightful, beautiful branches that he held alluringly in front of her and partly by sinking his teeth into one of her mittens and dragging with all his might. Of course, she had no idea of changing her mind and turning around to go home. When he had finally managed to capture one of her mittens, his joy was unbounded. He managed to get the mitten airborne, caught it again when it fell, and it was with the utmost difficulty that Cecilia persuaded him to give it back. Wildly he jumped and hopped around Cecilia's feet.

As soon as he understood that she had no intention of deserting him and that she was going to accompany him on a real promenade, he gradually quieted down. Now and then he went off into the ditch or among the hedges, following here one track, there another.

But he was careful not to disappear for any great length of time. The memory of his feeling of aloneness was still with him, and he kept a watchful eye on the girl who now represented his security and his god.

For this reason, Cecilia was doubly surprised when he suddenly disappeared and failed to return. She had kept a brisk pace; they had already reached the road below the school hill when it happened. Ramrod ducked in through a hole in the old, familiar hedge, not to be seen again.

Cecilia continued walking a number of yards down the road, preoccupied with her own thoughts, before she noticed that Ramrod had disappeared. At that point she stood and whistled—at first softly and a bit apathetically, then much more loudly, using the whistle she had so often heard Knut use. But Ramrod didn't return.

"Well, isn't that nice now if he has just taken off to heaven knows where?" Cecilia thought to herself. She had just begun to realize what a protective influence he was on a nocturnal promenade along deserted roads.

"Ramrod! Ramrod!"

There was a slight rustle from the other side of the hedge, but that was all.

Cecilia whistled again and, her heart beating anxiously, took a few additional steps along the road. At that point the hedge ended, and its place was taken by a jumble of broken, twisted barbed wire.

With a couple of quick, nimble hops, Cecilia cleared the ditch; one more hop, and she was over the fallen fence. From that point she would be able to see better into the vacant lot, almost up to the cellar and the place where the snowman stood.

The cellar!

Heavens! What if Ramrod had gone and fallen down into the hole. He was such a nosey dog; he wanted to examine everything in the world!

How cold and black were the frozen trees! The network of the branches was very much like the barbed wire—magnified, overgrown. It was the no man's land of deep winter. It was a dead vacant lot. . . .

"Ramrod! Ramrod!"

Uncertain of herself, Cecilia took a couple of slow steps into the drifts of snow. To one side she bent a low-lying bush—a bush that still had some small, hard red berries on it. They looked like drops of blood.

Cecilia peered among the trees and bushes. Quickly she oriented herself. Over there was the school; and there was the lumberyard; and there, in spite of the fact that new snow had fallen, were the hollows that were left by the snowballs they had rolled for their snowman.

It was amazing that she hadn't caught sight of the snowman as yet. After all, he was pretty tall, and his black round hat should have stood out in sharp contrast to all the whiteness.

173

Over there was the hill where the cellar was. By this time Cecilia was so close to it that she could see how tramped down the snow around it was.

But the snowman and his hat? She looked around searchingly, amazed.

Then a strange sound rose from the bushes. It was so close that Cecilia recoiled. At first it was weak, but it was in an even, low tone. Gradually it gained in strength, in anxiety, and in fright to become, at last, a lone, wild cry calculated to reach the stars.

It was Ramrod yowling, and the howl signified such intensive urgency that Cecilia put both hands to her face. She pressed her fingers against her forehead and tried to get her lips into the proper position to whistle.

She was not successful. They were too stiff—both from cold and from fright.

Her heart beating wildly, she went a little closer to the hill. Her eyes searched every inch of the territory around her. As yet, she had not discovered Ramrod, but suddenly, unexpectedly, she caught sight of something black and round—something that she had been looking for much higher up—the snowman's hat!

Without examining it, Cecilia picked it up. She was still eagerly peering in among the bushes.

As soon as she stopped looking for the hat as a landmark, she saw the snowman almost immediately. Although his head had been pushed a little to one side, his coal eyes stared vacantly and a bit squintingly out into the darkness, and his bald head shone, white and round, as if it were a satellite of the moon itself.

A shadow moved at the foot of the snowman. Ramrod!

He had ceased barking, but he was howling weakly, penetratingly. The sound was one that Knut often described as "Ramrod's screeches."

He was examining something large and dark that lay in the snow and was partially covered by it; it looked like an old pile of clothes.

Cecilia rushed forward. By now she had gotten so close that she could make out a lock or two of brown hair and the dark blue of a very familiar duffel coat.

Throwing the snowman's hat into the snow, she threw herself on her hands and knees beside the dark figure.

"Michael!" she screamed. "Michael!"

She threw all caution to the winds. Taking him by the shoulders, she shook him hard. She lifted his arms; she pulled on his hands.

But his limbs were lifeless and cold, and when she let go, they fell, with no control, into the loose, newly fallen snow.

For the first time in her life Cecilia experienced a sensation of absolute panic.

She looked around in all directions, as if she believed that the black trees could help her or perhaps the cold white moon, which was shining so unconcernedly on the roof of the school.

There was no one to sympathize except Ramrod; he stuck his nose in Michael's ear and snorted so loudly that bits of snow flew into the air.

It was a powerful snort; perhaps it reached all the way to Michael's inner ear. Suddenly his body moved jerkily.

At that point Cecilia sat down and moved cautiously toward him. Her actions were calm and purposeful now that she had seen him move. She lifted his head and placed it on her knee; her fingers brushed away the hair from his forehead. With long, even strokes, she rubbed a snowball along his temples.

Ramrod's eyes followed her every motion with deep interest. He lay down and placed his powerful head against Michael's shoulders.

A new spasm of movement went through the almost lifeless figure. His arms and legs began to move. The head on Cecilia's lap fell to one side. His colorless lips began to move.

Cecilia's heart was in her mouth. She had been scared out of her senses. Now she put one ear to his mouth. He looked as if he were trying to say something.

Finally he managed to make a sound. Cecilia was surprised to hear her own name.

"Quick. Quick . . . Cecie . . . the motor scooter . . ."

And finally, in a last desperate attempt: "The snowman . . . came to life . . . arrest him . . . go after the snowman . . ."

18

THE CONCLUSION

"And there they foun' him in th' snow, you see! She screamed—all girls scream—and shook him, but he was jus' like dead!"

Erik Acker was compelled to interrupt his story in order to catch his breath. His little brother Henrik took immediate advantage of this unexpected opportunity and broke in.

"He *was* dead—or at least almost! Both his arms and legs had had their heads cut off . . ."

The utterly enchanted listeners—a group of their playmates—were breathless and silent. It was a big thing for them to get hold of "inside information" about the drama that, by now, was the sole topic of conversation all over town.

Erik gave Henrik a devastating look.

"Aw," he hissed, "you haven't the slightest idea what

178

you're talking about. He *wasn't* dead, not really. They brought him to consciousness at the hospital later. But my sis thought he was dead clear up to the time he said the stuff about 'Go after the snowman!'"

The audience didn't take this latter very seriously. Per, Erik's best friend and severest critic, ran his fingers through his white-blond hair and expressed the feelings of them all.

"Aw, you can't kid me. The guy was out of his head. And it wasn't any old snowman who had hit him, either!"

"Yes, it was too!" Henrik trembled with excitement. His imagination, which had worked overtime, had caused the snowman to take on the proportions of an ogre, and in addition had endowed it with both life and breath and soul. "He had even taken off his hat, Cecie said . . ."

Erik, feeling that his prestige had been threatened, interrupted sharply.

"You keep quiet! You don't know a single thing about this, I can tell you!"

He took a long, deep breath.

"It's plain as day that he was out of his head—at least partly. But it wasn't totally his imagination! You remember that he had followed the thieves on the motor scooter, which he had decided to use. Of course they had found out he was around and had seen him, you see; and one of them, a big tough guy, had hidden behind the snowman! And when Michael got up close enough, he moved forward and clunked Michael!"

You could have heard a pin drop. Not even Henrik had any comments to make. Erik decided he could afford to lower his voice.

179

"Cecie, my sis, says that the guy—he's a brother of one of the girls in her class—had on one of those white jackets like they use up in the ski resorts. And it was for that reason that Michael thought the snowman himself had knocked him down. She remembered the white jacket afterwards when she saw the motor scooter. She recognized it and knew whose it was. She's awful smart, my sis!"

Erik's voice was filled with pride; this would have made Cecilia wide-eyed had she been there to hear it. However, he reminded himself just in time that he was talking about a sister—a *girl*, after all. Hastily he added, "At least once in a while."

He then continued: "And when Michael came to, he remembered the license number of the car. And of course they caught the thieves as easy as you please!"

Per, the one with the very light hair, slowly zipped and unzipped his jacket. His blue eyes, which at times could almost disappear in the wrinkles caused by his laughter, were now wide and serious. He seemed to be focusing on some far-distant point, beyond the snowman and the stolen goods, beyond the speeding cars, the desperate struggle.

"Hey, listen," he said. "That guy and his sister. The ones they caught. I know where they live. Evander is their name. And they have a huge, gigantic house and piles of spending money and a whole lot of cars and motor scooters and everything else you can imagine! Why did they go around robbing newsstands and stores when they could

180

buy anything in the world they wanted?"

"Jeepers," Henrik said in a shrill voice. "I wonder why they did do it?"

"Why did they do it?"

The words might well have been an echo. Miles from the place where Erik and Henrik and their friends asked the unanswerable question, the same words were being spoken.

It was Cecilia who had posed the question. She was sitting in a room on the fifth floor in one of the buildings of the brand-new City General Hospital; close by, in a white hospital bed with white sheets and blankets, was Michael. The only spot of color in the whole bed, for that matter, was his face, which, in spite of all the bandages, looked surprisingly healthy and sunburned.

Knut was there too. It was he who had suggested that they go to the hospital to see Michael.

"Oh, I wouldn't dare to go," Cecilia had answered without thinking.

"Dare?" Knut said in astonishment. "What are you afraid of? The hospital itself?"

Cecilia blushed. She didn't have the slightest idea what had made her answer him that way.

"Of course I'm not afraid!" she said angrily.

"Then I don't know why you're hesitating," Knut said in utter frankness. "Certainly you aren't afraid of Michael."

"You're just as crazy as ever," Cecilia answered illogically. "Well, O.K. I guess we might as well!"

After school they took the train. On the first floor of the hospital building they pooled their resources and bought three red cyclamens in the flower shop.

"The third one is from Ramrod," Knut said as he handed them to Michael.

Quickly Cecilia drew up a chair and sat down beside the bed. She was blushing clear up to the roots of her hair, partly because of the presence of three strange faces—one of them with a beard—that stared at her from the three other beds in the room, and partly because, as she had expected, it seemed strange to see Michael in bed and helpless.

Even Knut didn't have all his wits about him.

"Hey, are you sick?" he asked hastily.

That broke the ice. Both Michael and Cecilia had to smile.

"Why in the world do you think I'm here in this bed if I'm not sick?" Michael said with a big grin.

"You're so goofy, Knut," Cecilia said calmly. Normal color had returned to her face. In a moment or so, they were talking vigorously, just as usual.

At the first lull in the conversation, after Michael had described the events that had taken place on Saturday night, Cecilia posed her thoughtful, hesitant question.

"Why did they do it?"

"Well, for my part, I think it's absolutely ununderstandable!" Knut said. "Those kids. They have everything they've ever wanted or wished for—and then some!"

Michael cautiously moved his bandaged head on the pillow.

"Well, if you ask me," he said contemplatively, "I think you've hit on the reason right there. Don't you see? They have absolutely everything, and for that reason they feel that something is missing. Something all the rest of us have most of the time. Excitement. Enjoyment. The excitement that comes from wishing for something, working to save up enough money to get it . . ."

". . . to long for something . . ." Cecilia filled in.

"Yes, that's it! I finally understood—little by little—that the only thing Mary Beth really cared about and looked for was excitement. The excitement of riding, the thrill of driving at a wild speed, the fun of answering anything as impertinently as possible during school time, and, finally, the excitement of committing robberies and fooling the police."

"You know, I think you're right!" Knut said admiringly. "You were exciting to her, too. That's why she wanted to sink her hooks into you!"

The ceiling light seemed mercilessly strong as a deep silence fell over the group. One of the other patients rustled his newspaper. Knut hastily deserted the realm of speculation; he really wasn't much at home there.

"Actually, I was the one who was responsible for their being caught," he remarked in an exaggerated tone of bravery and pride. "I was the one who hit on the idea of building a snowman!"

"Oh, sure," Cecilia said sarcastically. "You're the one, all right! You suggested the snowman because you noticed that Mary Beth was trying to entice Michael over to her

184

house. She was the one who set the trap for herself. That's how it *really* was!"

"You're right," Michael responded. "I think she did set a trap for herself. I think most people do in situations like this. . . . And you know, there's something else I've been thinking about, too. I don't know exactly how to explain it, but it's different with different people. Some people— in fact, most people—don't have anything to do with lying or stealing or such things because they know that it isn't right. At least, I feel that that's true. They simply don't have any desire to indulge in such things. Some others don't mess around with such things because they know they might be caught, because they're afraid of the police, afraid of the teacher, or afraid of someone. But that kind gets involved much more easily."

Suddenly Cecilia giggled.

"Well, you certainly don't belong to that second group," she said. "Because you did something completely insane on Saturday night. But since you didn't once think either about the law or the police, I don't think it has even oc- curred to you."

Michael and Knut both stared at her in astonishment.

"I did?" Michael said, lifting his head from the pillow and letting it sink down almost immediately again because of the pain. "I did? What do you mean?"

"You . . . stole . . . Mary Beth's . . . motor scooter!" Cecilia said slowly and dramatically.

"Aw, that's nothing. He could have borrowed that any old time he wanted to," Knut said. "Anyway, she has it back now."

185

"And that wasn't the worst thing," Cecilia continued, not once taking her eyes off the sunburned face buried in the bandages. "In addition, you rode it, Michael! All around half of Nordvik. And you aren't even fifteen years old yet!"

Again there was silence—such a silence that the other patients in the room began to be interested and looked over toward Michael's bed. The man with the newspaper took off his glasses and cleaned them in order that he might see more clearly.

Knut laughed and cleared the air.

"Ha, ha, ha! That's a hot one. Now Inspector Nilsson will have to put his fair-haired boy in jail!"

Michael looked completely crestfallen. For a few seconds his mouth was wide open. He hadn't looked that way since he was in the first grade.

"I . . . I never thought of that!" he said. "It never once occurred to me. It's as simple as that. Good heavens! Did they say anything? The police, I mean?"

"Not that I know of." Cecilia giggled. "Maybe it will never occur to them, either. Or if it does, I doubt that they'll do anything. What I mean is that you certainly don't belong to the second group you were talking about —the ones who are just concerned with laws and police without having any idea what's right and wrong. . . . Because what you did was right in any case . . . !"

"There's no question about that. It was absolutely right!" Knut confirmed. "And it was a lucky thing for the police that you did what you did. They were about to make a terrible mistake!"

"Like what, for instance?" Michael said in surprise.

Cecilia looked him in the eye.

"They were going to arrest your friend at the lumber-yard yesterday," she said in a hushed voice. "Among other things for a robbery that took place in a villa up in Lindeby one night a while back. They had found out that he was up there with some pals dancing that particular night. And then if we had come along and told the police about the cellar and all the stolen goods, right there so close to where he worked . . ."

Michael didn't move a muscle as he stared straight up at the ceiling. It looked as if he weren't stopping with the ceiling but were, instead, staring straight through it.

"Lindeby," he said slowly. "Lindeby . . ."

"Yes," Cecilia said so calmly that Knut glanced at her anxiously. "In Lindeby. They've admitted everything with no fuss—both Peter and Fighter. They had to because they had a cupboard full of liquor and other things from that Lindeby house down in the cellar. It was that same night—you know, Michael . . ." Her voice died away, but with superhuman effort she managed to regain her power of speech. Her voice became a little hoarse as she said, "They rode back up there after they took you home."

"Mary Beth, too?"

"Mary Beth, too."

Once more Cecilia and Michael looked deeply into each other's eyes.

Ill at ease, Knut squirmed.

"It was pretty quiet in class today," he said. He simply had to say something. "Mary Beth has quit."

Suddenly a bell rang, long, monotonously, continuously.

"Heavens, do they have bells here, too?"

"I'm afraid that they're ringing us out!" Knut said as he arose. "End of visiting hours, you see. Look, Michael. We'll come see you soon again. By the way, is there anything you want us to bring you?"

Michael almost managed to sit up.

"Jeepers, I'll say there is. I'm glad you asked. Look, go get my textbooks—the whole bunch of them—and find out what the assignments are when you bring them!"

With a look of incredulity, Knut stared at Michael's bandaged head and then at the angry red temperature chart at the end of the bed.

"What a mountain climb on that chart!" he said. "You can't tell me you're going to study!"

"My temperature was almost normal at one o'clock," Michael sputtered. "Of course, it's gone up now since you've been here."

The door to the room opened and a nurse entered. Her healthy pink cheeks were a sharp contrast to her well-starched professional clothing. Meaningfully, she stood there holding the door open as she looked all around the room.

For a second she was almost unprofessional as her eyes focused on the three heads so close to each other.

"I'm going to plug away at my studies. Nothing else!" Michael explained. "I've just got to get my job back at the lumberyard as soon as I can get out of here!"

"Visiting hours are over!" the nurse said.

"So long, Michael!"

"Bye, now."

They filed past the nurse. In the doorway Cecilia's small figure was overshadowed by Knut's tall dark one.

The nurse saw the expression on Michael's face.

"Very soon," she thought. "It won't be long before it's you who will be following her. Right at her heels."